"I'm no good for you," Jeffrey said, "no good at settling down...."

"Have I asked you to?"

He'd never heard a voice so cold. "You're angry with me. All I wanted was for you to understand...."

"And I do." Susanna gave him a sad smile. "I really do. And I thank you for everything you've given me. Sincerely. I will always be in your debt."

"Don't." He caught her hands. "I don't want us to part this way. Susanna," he said urgently, "remember what we said before?"

She nodded, blinking back tears.

"Friends, remember?"

"Yes," she whispered huskily, nodding again. "Friends." Raising up, she kissed his cheek, then tugged free of his hands and stepped back. "I'm afraid friendship is no longer enough for me, however. I'm sorry.... Goodbye, Jeffrey."

Wanting to stop her, knowing he couldn't, Jeffrey stood and watched the woman he loved walk out of his life.

Dear Reader,

These days, when it feels like winter just *might* last forever, don't forget—you can find all the warmth and magic of springtime anytime in a Silhouette Romance book.

Each month, Silhouette Romance brings you six captivating love stories. Share all the laughter, the tears and the tenderness as our spirited heroines and irresistible heroes discover the wonder and power of love.

This month, meet the dynamic Thatcher Brant, hero of *Haunted Husband*. The handsome widower has vowed he'll never love again. But Samantha Hogan is determined to break the spell of Thatcher's past and win his heart. It all happens in Elizabeth August's SMYTHESHIRE, MASSACHUSETTS, a small New England town with big secrets....

Thatcher is also a FABULOUS FATHER, part of our special series about very special dads.

Then there's *Sally's Beau,* Riley Houston. He's the footloose and fancy-free type, but Sally's out to show Riley there's world enough for this pair of ALL-AMERICAN SWEETHEARTS in Paradise Falls, West Virginia! Don't miss this heartwarming story from Laurie Paige.

Rounding out the month, there's Carla Cassidy's *The Golden Girl,* Gayle Kaye's *Hard Hat and Lace,* Val Whisenand's *Daddy's Back* and Anne Peters's sophisticated *The Pursuit of Happiness.*

In the coming months, we'll be bringing you books by all your favorite authors—Diana Palmer, Annette Broadrick, Suzanne Carey and more!

I hope you enjoy this book, and all the stories to come.

Happy Reading!

Anne Canadeo
Senior Editor

THE PURSUIT OF HAPPINESS

Anne Peters

Silhouette
R O M A N C E™
Published by Silhouette Books New York
America's Publisher of Contemporary Romance

SILHOUETTE BOOKS
300 E. 42nd St., New York, N.Y. 10017

THE PURSUIT OF HAPPINESS

ISBN: 0-373-08927-9

First Silhouette Books printing March 1993

Printed in the U.S.A.

Books by Anne Peters

Silhouette Romance

Through Thick and Thin #739
Next Stop: Marriage #803
And Daddy Makes Three #821
Storky Jones Is Back in Town #850
Nobody's Perfect #875
The Real Malloy #899
The Pursuit of Happiness #927

Silhouette Desire

Like Wildfire #497

ANNE PETERS

makes her home in the Pacific Northwest with her husband and their dog, Adrienne. Family and friends, reading, writing and travel—those are the things she loves most. Not always in that order, not always with equal fervor, but always without exception.

Washington, D.C.
21 July

Dearest Maria,

How I miss you. I've only been away from you a
month—a much shorter separation than others we've
endured—yet it seems like forever. An entire ocean, a
world, lies between us. It keeps us apart in a way poli-
tics, an Iron Curtain or the Berlin Wall never could. . . .

I love you always, remember that. . . .

Yours,
Harry

Chapter One

"Excuse me, Miss—"

Susanna opened her eyes. Momentarily disori-
ented, she blinked against the glare of sunshine in the
aircraft cabin.

A flight attendant was leaning over her with a smile
of apology. "I believe you wanted some aspirin?"

"Oh, yes." Rousing herself, Susanna cupped a
palm. "Thank you." She tossed back the pills with a
grimace of distaste and quickly washed them down
with the proffered water. "Thank you very much,"
she repeated gratefully, taking care to pronounce the
difficult *th* sound just so. "I believe I'll try to sleep a
little."

"Best thing for a headache," the attendant con-
curred. "How about some eyeshades?"

Susanna frowned, puzzled. "I beg your pardon. Eye—?"

"Shades," the man next to her in the aisle seat supplied helpfully. *"Verdunkelung."* He gestured to his steel-rimmed glasses. *"Versteh?"*

Surprised by the intrusion, Susanna shifted her gaze to his. The man's German was fractured, to be sure, but yes, she had understood. She asked him, *"Sie sprechen Deutsch?"*

He shook his head, his grin ruefully charming. "Not nearly as well as you seem to speak English."

"Oh." Disconcerted by the openly thorough way the man studied her face, and by the gleam that began to sparkle in his narrowed green eyes, Susanna quickly returned her attention back to the still hovering stewardess. "Some, uh, shades would be nice, thank you."

"I'll be right back."

The attendant left and Susanna settled back in her seat. She closed her eyes.

"Headache, huh?"

Her neighbor again. Susanna really did not care to talk. "Hmm." She kept her eyes closed, hoping he would take the hint.

He didn't. "Let me know if the aspirin doesn't do it for you," he persisted. "I've got something more potent in my briefcase you're welcome to have."

Something more potent . . . A frisson of apprehension made Susanna tense. Could this man possibly be one of those American gangsters she had occasionally seen portrayed in films?

With pretended casualness, she rolled her head to one side and studied him through lowered lashes.

Hair, reddish brown, wavy and on the long side. Eyes, cool and green as mint behind those steel-rimmed spectacles. Shifty? His face was in profile, so Susanna couldn't tell. She did think, however, that her earlier glimpse of the narrow slash of his nose and the thin-lipped mouth had made him seem sufficiently ruthless to be—possibly . . .

He caught her looking.

Flushing, Susanna faced forward. "A-aspirin will be *gut genug*," she stammered, her facility in English a casualty to rattled nerves. *"Danke."*

His amused, "You're welcome," made her flush even more. No doubt the man had misinterpreted her prolonged glance and fancied she found him attractive. Which, she reluctantly conceded, he was, in a quietly dangerous sort of way.

She certainly envied him the ease with which he conducted himself. It left her without a doubt that this was not the first trip in an airplane *he* had ever taken. He had the look of a seasoned traveler; at least, how Susanna imagined a seasoned traveler would look. Comfortable, relaxed, wearing jeans that were soft and faded from many washings, and with the bare foot attached to a bony ankle resting on one knee shod in equally supple-looking leather. A black sweater, sleeves bunched near his elbows, draped the slouching curve of his torso with negligent ease. It was made of wool the texture of which, when she had inadvertently touched it, had reminded Susanna of the velvet drapes in Comrade *Bürgermeister*'s overstuffed office: a luxuriant softness, a decadent sort of elegance.

No doubt it was cashmere, Susanna mused, but it might as well have been spun gold for all the kinship that kind of wool had to the scratchy stuff of her own preunification gray suit. And stuffed into the overhead compartment, next to her own serviceable raincoat, was the man's suede leather jacket.

Whatever his field—perhaps gangster, though probably not—the man exuded an air of affluence the way winter coats in Linzberg gave off the smell of mothballs.

Clothes had always been way down on Susanna's list of priorities. Not that she didn't like them, not that she didn't try to make the most of the few she had—there just had never been the money. She had saved every *Pfennig* she possibly could for this very trip, long before she had dared to think the dream might actually become a reality. Long before the rumblings of discontent in East Germany had become thunderous outcries, she had fantasized about this day, this flight. Long before the Berlin Wall and all it symbolized had been hacked to pieces and the people behind it set free, she had prayed for freedom such as this.

She'd scrimped and saved, dreamed, hoarded and planned for what seemed like forever to her. In fact, it had only been some seventeen years since her mother had died, leaving the letters and the locket for Susanna, and taking away with her the only love Susanna had ever received.

But Maria had left her daughter hope, too. Hope of leaving one day; hope of arriving.

And now, finally, incredibly, that day was at hand. She was on an airplane. She was on her way to...America.

America. One small word for so many hopes. So many dreams. Yet now that she was halfway there, to

Susanna it suddenly seemed like the most frightening word in the language she had so diligently studied.

Anxiety, panic, all the doubts and misgivings that had been momentarily diverted by her contemplation of her seatmate, now clutched anew at her heart. The pounding in her head intensified. She squeezed her eyes shut and stifled a gasp.

"Here you are, miss." The attendant's arrival was timely. Susanna gratefully accepted the eyeshades and, putting them on, endeavored to shut out the world.

She must have dozed. Crazy thoughts and visions tumbled through her head in multicolored fragments, as though viewed through the peephole of a kaleidoscope. The hum of hundreds of conversations faded away, as did her awareness of the man in the next seat. Yet when she started in response to a slight touch on her shoulder, she was instantly awake.

Aircraft, she thought. America. And she sat up on a surge of anticipation—and fear.

No time to dwell on it, though. The touch on her shoulder firmed. "Miss," she was told with professional solicitude, "we'll be serving lunch shortly. Perhaps food will help you get rid of your headache."

Susanna groped for the shades, pushing them up and onto her forehead. "My head is much better, thank you." It was wonderful to be able to say so truthfully. "And I *am* hungry."

She straightened and in so doing belatedly realized that she'd been nestled against her neighbor's side. "I beg your pardon," she murmured, hot with embarrassment.

"Not at all." That smile again. "Glad I was able to help."

"Help?" she repeated, at a loss. The man had a way of appraising her that seriously impaired her mental faculties.

"In ridding you of your headache."

"Oh." His smile exposed teeth whiter and more even than any she had ever seen.

His chuckle drew her gaze upward. Laughter lurked in his eyes, too, and the heat in her cheeks intensified. He must think her a proper fool, Susanna thought crossly, and looked away with a forced little laugh. "As you can see, I don't wake up too bright."

"Bright enough." He eyed her with interest. "You're from the other side, aren't you?" he questioned, adding, "This your first trip abroad?"

Was it so obvious? Susanna tugged at the jacket of her tailored wool suit, saw the signs of wear at the cuffs, the age-imbedded creases in the skirt, and admitted it was. She nodded without looking at him.

"You have family in the States?"

Astonishment at what she considered a very personal question made Susanna give him a frown. "Why do you ask?"

Where she came from, it had not been that long since questions of any kind, no matter how seemingly innocuous, could wreak havoc if carelessly answered.

Her neighbor shrugged, his expression bland. "Just making conversation."

"Oh." Susanna relaxed as much as she could, given the man's intensive perusal and her overall anxiety. "I, uh, I hope to have."

"Hope to have?" Auburn brows arched. "Pardon me, but what the hell does that mean?"

"I have an address."

"I see." He pursed his lips. "And did you write to that address, Miss, er, Mrs . . . ?"

"Jaeger," Susanna replied absently. "No, I didn't. I . . . That is, my visit will be a, you know . . . a . . . surprise." The word finally came to her. Actually, she'd been afraid to write and announce herself because . . . Well, what if she hadn't been wanted? The disappointment would have been more than she could have borne after all the years of dreaming. This way, once she was here in the flesh . . .

"A surprise, eh?" Her neighbor gave a soundless whistle. "You've got guts, Ms. Jaeger."

"Guts?"

"Nerve." He grinned. "You know, courage."

"Ah." She smiled as she understood, but honesty compelled her to shake her head. "But no, Mr . . ."

"Kent. Jeffrey Kent."

"Mr. Kent. I have none of what you call guts at all. All I have is hope, really, and quite a lot of afraid."

"Fear," he corrected quietly, his gaze hooded by a gathering frown.

"Yes." Susanna nodded, that very emotion threatened to close her throat. "Fear."

There weren't a great many things Jeffrey Alan Kent had ever feared in his life. Apart from his father's wrath as a boy, that was, and maybe the ire of his high school football coach. He had gone into many foreign countries without knowing anyone there; he was a journalist. Traveling where no man—or, at least, no competing pressman—had gone before was what his job as a foreign correspondent for one of the big wire services was all about. But to set out blindly, alone, in the hope of locating a relative, as this quite appealing Miss or Mrs. Jaeger with the wild, black Gypsy hair and drab, shapeless suit seemed to be doing...

Jeff shook his head. Uh-uh. He wouldn't want to do it. The fact that this woman *was* doing it spoke volumes about the kind of life she was leaving behind. It touched him.

Jeff didn't want to be touched. After a long and grueling stint covering the Persian Gulf and the Middle East, he had had it up to the eyeballs with suffering humanity and heartrending stories. He was done with that. He was on vacation; with luck, a long one. He was looking forward to beer with the guys and Monday night football. And to some healthy, uncomplicated...flirtations with a string of homegrown beauties.

Lunch arrived. Checking it out, Jeff grimaced. Steak like leather; it figured. Likewise, a cardboard roll, limp vegetables, gray pasta. Airline fare! He desultorily picked at his meal and fantasized about his mother's home cooking. He glanced at his watch. Just three more hours.

"This is sooo delicious."

Startled by his neighbor's incongruous remark, Jeff turned his head. Ms. Jaeger was chewing enthusiastically, with obvious enjoyment.

"I still find it difficult," she said, "to believe everyone can eat like this—" she gestured toward their trays "—every day!" She eyed his untouched roll. "You are not eating your bread?"

"No, I...I'm not very hungry." Some unwelcome emotion, all but unrecognizable from years of disuse, but suspiciously akin to shame, made it impossible for Jeff to say what he really thought of the food. He caught her gaze and got the message. "If you'd like to have it...?"

Her smile, the first genuine one he had seen on her face, was like a gift. One he didn't feel he deserved, given the modest nature of his offering, but one he accepted with pleasure, nonetheless.

"Thank you," she said, and her smile broadened when he passed over his pat of butter and hunk of carrot cake, too. "But are you sure?" propriety seemed to prompt her to say.

Jeff grinned, touched again, but not minding it this time. "Positive."

He watched her dig in, daintily, but with the kind of single-mindedness only people who have hungered bring to the table. Somehow it made him want to defend his own lack of appetite. "I, er, I'm saving my stomach for my mother's apple pie."

"Hmm?" Chewing, she attentively arched brows that were as black as crow's wings. Her eyes were black, too, and as deep as a bottomless lake. A man could easily drown in them.

Suddenly aware that she had spoken, Jeff sharply recalled himself. "I'm sorry, you were saying...?"

Quickly shaking her head, she pointedly swallowed, then took a sip of coffee. Dabbing her mouth with her napkin, she said, "I'm sorry. People with accents should not speak with their mouths full. I merely wondered, other than your mother, do you have family in Seattle?"

She pronounced it "Seetle," the way Jeff had heard other foreigners do. He corrected her, approving her second attempt with a nod as he added, "Yes. I grew up there, you see. It's my home."

"Ah."

She ate some more with obvious enjoyment. He watched. At length she said wistfully, "Homes are important, aren't they?"

"I suppose. To some people. Personally, I'm content to roam the world and lay my head wherever the next story takes me."

"Story?"

"I'm a political reporter...."

"Ah."

"On international assignments for the past six years."

"I see." She sipped daintily at her coffee, into which, Jeff noted with amusement, she had dumped three packs of sugar. It seemed the lady had a sweet tooth. "And you like what you do?"

"Very much. I wouldn't be caught dead stuck behind some desk or living in one place—" He interrupted himself. She was looking bewildered again. "What?"

"'Caught dead'?" she queried, frowning.

He laughed. "An expression. Not to be taken literally. Means I need action, excitement. I need to keep moving. You know?"

"No." She neatly aligned her cutlery at right angles to the rectangular plastic plate on which the entrée had been served, the smile she gave him almost apologetic. "I'm afraid I don't. To keep moving is the very last thing *I* have ever wished to do. Including this journey to America, I have relocated three times, and to me that is two times too many."

"Yes, well..." Jeff stretched and stifled a yawn. "Different strokes and all that," he added. "So where was home originally?"

She measured him with a glance. "Linzberg. It's a rather small town in southeastern Germany. In the province of Thüringen. Do you know of it?"

"The province, vaguely. We call it Thuringia. Is your family still there?"

"No." Abruptly the reserve was back.

"I'm sorry." Jeff folded his napkin, just as she was doing, and tossed it onto his tray. "If I've intruded..."

She shook her head quickly, making her curls bounce. "It's all right." She sighed. Her eyes were clouded; pain lurked in their inky depths. "They're all dead, you see."

"I'm sorry."

Her smile was sad. "I am, as well." Taking a deep breath, she visibly bucked herself up. "I have lived in Berlin these past several years and so I was, as I believe you say, John on the spot—"

"Johnny," Jeff corrected. "The expression is '*Johnny*-on-the-spot.'"

"Of course. Johnny." Susanna shrugged, her smile turning wry. "I have tried very much to learn the correct colloquialisms, but..." She shrugged again. "It's confusing, yes?"

"Definitely." Jeff chuckled. "What's more, the slang of the day changes so quickly, it's impossible to keep up with it unless you're a teenager, so don't sweat it."

"Don't sweat...ah." Susanna nodded; understanding dawned. "Slang again, right?"

"Right. And it means don't worry about it. At least, it used to last time I was home. Like as not, by now it's a completely outdated phrase. I haven't been home for a while, you see, so I can't be sure."

"Ah." Susanna nodded again. "In any case, I was in the right place at the right time when the Wall came down."

"And so you were able to leave."

"Yes." Falling silent, she looked out the window.

Following suit, Jeff looked at the puffs of white clouds that looked like huge, billowing down comforters and marveled at the lengths people were willing to go to in order to be free. This young woman had no one in the whole world and, judging by her clothing, she had only limited funds. Yet here she was, putting everything on the line in the hope of finding—what? Relatives who might or might not be happy to be surprised by someone they had never clapped eyes on or heard of before.

Troubled, he shifted his gaze to the fall of black curls at the back of his seatmate's head. She had gathered their abundance into a haphazard sort of ponytail, and its ends fell below her shoulders. He pictured it loose, imagined its texture. . . .

When she suddenly turned and their eyes met, he was embarrassed. Without thinking, he blurted, "You have wonderful hair."

Obviously taken aback, she blushed. "I . . . It's a family trait, I suppose."

"On your mother's side?" Why was he asking?

"No, my mother was a blonde." Still visibly disconcerted, Susanna fussed with her tray. "I wish they would come and collect these."

* * *

Their conversation more or less ground to a halt after that. The meal over and trays removed, Ms. Jaeger pulled out a dog-eared copy of *Time* magazine and buried her nose in it. Jeff took that as a hint to leave her alone.

Actually, Susanna began to read because she still found it difficult to maintain the casually open tone that perfect strangers used with each other in the West. Americans, especially, were reputed to be instantly friendly and warmly outgoing and this...this Mr. Kent had certainly proven that to be the case.

Watching his tall, lean, broad-shouldered form make its way up the jetway into Seattle's Sea-Tac Airport, Susanna experienced a momentary sense of loss. He had been the first American with whom she had had a chance to converse. Beset by fear and trepidation about all the uncertainties that awaited her, she prayed that everyone else might be as pleasant as he had been.

Habit had her tensing at the sight of uniforms. But the immigration and customs officers were gruffly kind. Her papers were in order; her visa granted her a six-week stay in the U.S. All too soon, it seemed, she found herself on the other side of some doors, surrounded by throngs of hugging, chatting and smiling people.

No one was there for her. But then, no one knew she was coming.

Lost, she searched the crowd for Mr. Kent's tall form. There he was on the fringe, waiting for what Susanna soon realized was a train. Reassured by the sight of him, she allowed the crowd to sweep her along and aboard.

They met again on the covered sidewalk outside the terminal. It was cold and damp; drizzling rain made the concrete walls of the parking garage across the street as gray and drab as Susanna knew her suit to be. Uncertain as to how to proceed, and feeling chilled, she pulled on her worn raincoat and looked around for a taxi.

"Where are you headed?"

Mr. Kent's voice. Susanna sagged with relief. "Into Seattle."

Jeff was touched again by the careful way she pronounced it, just the way he had said it for her. He had watched her emerge from the building, observed the way she anxiously took her bearings. And though he'd told himself not to get involved, here he was, about to stick his neck out.

"It so happens," he said, "that I'm going there, too."

He raised an arm, and Susanna was impressed to see a very large sedan move forward instantly. "Taxis charge an arm and a leg . . ."

Another colloquialism, Susanna figured. Not to be taken literally.

" . . . so let's you and me share one, okay?"

"Yes, thank you." At that point, Susanna was so overwhelmed by all the newness, she would have agreed to anything as long as she didn't have to handle it alone.

"Seattle," Jeff told the driver after they had stowed their stuff in the trunk and gotten settled in the back seat. "Where exactly?" he asked Susanna.

She fumbled in her purse and handed him an obviously much-handled envelope. "It's right there in the corner."

"Hmm." Jeff briefly studied the letter's return address. "That'd be West Seattle, I'd say. Which means you get out first." He gave the driver instructions, then, handing the letter back to Susanna, asked, "Who lives there? An aunt? Uncle? Cousin?"

Susanna hesitated before answering. She bit her lip and finally said, "My... my father lives there. Actually."

Her *father*. The plot thickens, Jeff thought, and immediately reminded himself he was on vacation. There was no story here, and even if there was, someone else would have to write it.

All too soon, as far as Susanna was concerned, the cab pulled up at an old-fashioned house, its coat of white paint no longer fresh, on a street lined with houses of similar style and condition.

"Number 3521, ma'am," the driver announced. "That'll be $24.50."

Susanna barely heard what he said. She sat trapped in a maelstrom of emotions that made her regret having accepted and eaten her seatmate's dinner roll and cake. Both now threatened to make a return visit. She inhaled deeply, staring at the house. How different it looked from what she had envisioned. At once more neglected and shabbier with its coat of peeling whitewash, yet, fronted by a large expanse of lawn, larger and grander, too. Faced with the reality, her dreams and plans seemed foolhardy...

What was she doing here, she asked herself on a surge of panic, in this strange and overwhelming country, where the only person she knew at all was the man who was now gently urging her out of the taxi? What if . . . ? No. She would not give in to negative thoughts at this stage.

Forcing a smile, Susanna took the hand Jeff held out and let him help her to alight. The driver had taken her suitcase out of the trunk and set it upon the sidewalk, right next to a clump of grass growing out of some cracks. Similar clumps sprouted from similar cracks in similarly neglected sidewalks where she came from. Susanna took heart. Perhaps things weren't so very different here, after all.

She opened her handbag. "How much did you say?"

"Don't worry about it." A large hand covered hers. A charming smile met her glance of surprise. "It'll be my treat."

"But Mr. Kent—"

"Jeff," he interrupted, firming his grip so that her hand was trapped in the purse. "You're in America now and we're not so formal, Mrs. Jaeger."

"Miss," she corrected. Responding to his warmth, she added, "Not so formally, it would be Susanna."

Her eyes met his and lingered. She felt her smile begin to fade, giving way to a jolt of awareness which Jeff was the first to cut short.

He noisily cleared his throat and glanced toward the house. "Well, Susanna," he said, "I guess this is it, then. Your new home." He stepped back, half raising his hand in a gesture of farewell. "Good luck."

"Thank you." It was difficult to speak, Susanna found. Her throat had closed. She felt as if she were losing her last, her only, friend.

She turned abruptly and walked up to the house. At the front door she took a deep breath, held it a moment to slow her runaway pulse, and pressed the buzzer. As footsteps approached and a woman's voice called, "Coming," she turned to look back at the taxi.

Mr. Kent—Jeff—was leaning out of an open window, his face a question. How kind, Susanna thought, choking up again. He had waited to see if anyone was home.

She forced a smile and waved, nodding. He responded with a jaunty thumbs-up and then, as Susanna turned back to the opening door, the taxi sped away with impatiently squealing tires.

"Yes?" The middle-aged woman confronting Susanna was neither friendly nor otherwise.

Susanna offered her a nervous smile. "I beg your pardon," she said, moistening lips that were suddenly parched. "I wonder, is Joseph Harrison Miller at home?"

The woman blinked, then frowned. "Who?"

"J-Joseph . . ." Susanna faltered, a terrible sense of foreboding settled on her shoulders like a cape made of lead. Please, this could not be happening. She tried again. "Joseph Harrison—"

"Look, miss." The woman stepped back. "You got the wrong house."

"No, please." Susanna pressed a palm against the door to keep it from closing. She held out the letter she was clutching in her other hand. "I have it right here, #3521 Harborview Street. . . ."

"There's no Joseph Harrison here," the woman said firmly. "Nor Miller, either. Never was, that I know of." And she just as firmly closed the door.

Staring at the aged panel, her mind boggling as the immensity of her folly sank in, Susanna raised her hand to knock again. There had to be some mistake; he had to be there. The letter said...

The letter is thirty years old, Susanna.

A rush of expelled air tripped over a stifled sob, and Susanna let her hand drop. She turned blindly to go.

Washington, D.C.
8 September

My beloved Maria,

Though I am back in the country that I love, though I am home, I think of you and long for you every day....

You're pregnant! Maria, dearest, how could you have dared let it happen when you knew I would not be able to be there for you? I cannot come to you, nor you to me. Are you well? I worry....

How I wish I could hold you in my arms and feel the child—our child—grow inside you. It is flesh of my flesh, as you are the love of my life....

Always,
Harry

Chapter Two

No doubt about it, it was great to be home.

Flat on his back on the Murphy bed, arms folded behind his head, Jeffrey Kent listened to the wind whistling around the corners of the garage. With each gust of the howling wind, rain pelted the windows, sounding pretty much like the sandstorms he had been through in the Middle Eastern desert. But even with his eyes closed, half-asleep, he knew this was different. This was home.

Eyelids still heavy, Jeff surveyed the spacious room, taking pleasure in the helter-skelter of possessions that furnished the loft atop his parents' garage. He'd appropriated and converted it into his very own pad years ago. Six years, to be exact. Just before his first overseas assignment, and just after his brief, disastrous and never-to-be-repeated excursion into married domesticity had ended in divorce.

Single again, and itching to trade Seattle and personal failure for exotic places and professional success, he'd nevertheless seemed to need the assurance of having roots somewhere, of permanence. To him the word was synonymous with Mom and Dad and the house in which they'd raised him. And since they could well use the money he'd be paying them for rent and caretaking, the garage apartment had been a godsend all around.

It was good knowing he could follow his pursuits without having to worry about the place during his absences, too. Mom, bless her, kept everything spick-and-span and his scruffy houseplants watered. Yeah... Jeff's gaze traveled the eclectic decor of his home with pleasure.

Primitive masks rubbed elbows here with aboriginal totems, pottery vessels and a sculpture or two of questionable worth and authenticity. No matter, he loved them. Scores of framed photographs of his travels hung cheek by jowl with paintings he had picked up from sidewalk artists the world over. Some he liked because they were excellent, some precisely because they were awful. All of them had something special that set them apart from the ordinary.

Of all the things Jeff despised, ordinariness ranked top of the list. Broccoli came next.

So his home might not be an interior designer's idea of good taste and compatibility, but to him it was a visual record of all the special, *un*ordinary things he had done and seen. His exotic mementos of foreign places were interspersed with such things as high school yearbooks, a grimy catcher's mitt and mask, a #9—his number—football jersey, swim team trophies and other collectibles from his youth. Looking around at all of them reinforced the pleasure of being back home.

Snug in his bed, his favorite dinner still comfortably filling his stomach, the idea of permanently retiring his passport and suitcase momentarily gained in appeal. Maybe it was time he took O'Connell at the *Seattle Post-Intelligencer* up on his offer; maybe it was time to settle down, get a life.

He shifted onto his side. On the other hand, he'd had such inclinations at the end of difficult assignments before. And always, after a few weeks of R and R, the itch to get moving generally returned in epidemic proportions. This time'd be no different.

Still drowsing over his options, Jeff went back to sleep.

Susanna hadn't slept a wink, though she was tired to the point of exhaustion and emotionally drained. Just outside her window was the sign flashing the impressive name of Miranda Court Hotel. All through the long, stormy night she had lain on the bed fully dressed and watched the alternating red, white and green flash of neon make psychedelic patterns on the ceiling.

The place wasn't much, but it was cheap, and that was what counted, given her limited finances. She had indicated as much to the police officer who had seen her walking along the street with her suitcase last night. When he'd pulled up beside her, she had been frightened at first, thinking he intended to arrest her for loitering or something. But the officer had been very kind, and after she'd explained her predicament, he had driven her to this hotel in his patrol car.

The room cost fifteen dollars a night. But though the policeman had said this was a very reasonable price, it was money Susanna could ill afford to spend for very long.

Dry-eyed and despairing, she stared at the ceiling. The garish slashes of neon were less vivid now as the blackness of night gave way to a gray, wet and windy dawn. How, she asked herself for the millionth time, how could all of her dreams have been dashed so thoroughly, so quickly? And what, for the love of heaven, was she to do now? Where was she to go from here? Back?

Susanna shuddered. Back to what? There was no-where. No one. She had no home. The state had evicted her from the apartment in Linzberg she'd shared with her stepfather, Thomas Jaeger, within a month of his death nine years ago. She'd been told that, with huge numbers of families always waiting for adequate housing, wasting an entire apartment on one single person was out of the question.

Completely on her own then—her mother had succumbed to melancholy and a bout of pneumonia eight years before that when Susanna had been just thirteen—she had moved to Berlin. The Wall was still firmly in place, a move to the West an impossible dream, dreamed by many but realized by few. Still, she had felt that opportunities of any kind were bound to be better in the large, divided city than in the small town of Linzberg in the East German hinterland where she'd been born.

All she had taken with her were the letters from the man who was her father. And the locket.

Susanna fingered the small golden heart that nestled between her breasts. Over the years it had become a talisman of sorts, a good-luck charm, as well as a tangible symbol of the dream she had sworn to fulfill—the dream that had been her mother's as well as her own. Touching the locket never failed to bring that dream into focus, and once again she drew a measure of reassurance from the heart's warm smoothness.

She had found work in Berlin, pleased to find that nurses with operating-room experience were relatively well paid. She had lived simply, even more simply than conditions made it necessary for everybody to live. She had saved her money. She had studied and learned until she spoke the language of the letters—English—almost flawlessly.

And she had worn the locket, cherishing it as a legacy from her mother, all the while planning for the day when she would meet the man whose likeness was paired with Maria's inside the golden heart: Joseph Harrison Miller.

Susanna covered her burning eyes with one arm. The day of that long-awaited meeting had come and gone—and Joseph Harrison Miller was still just a name on some yellowing old letters.

Renewed despair had unshed tears pooling in her throat where they burned and almost choked her. What on earth was she to do now? She was alone in a land so overwhelmingly foreign that she might as well be on the moon. She knew no one.

No one. Except Jeffrey Kent.

Briefly she recalled the smile that had so effectively changed the expression of Jeffrey Kent's narrow features from ferocious to friendly. And she sensed that, despite her fanciful imaginings about his profession, and despite the disquieting effect the man had on her, he was someone who would come to her aid if she asked him. Had he not done so in letting her share the taxi? Had he not waited in front of the Miller house— at least, what she'd thought to be the Miller house— until he was certain she would be all right?

Where would she reach him, though? How could she find him?

Squelching the inner voice that said it was wrong to burden a complete stranger with her problems, Susanna tried to think. In her home country it would have been easy to locate someone—every citizen was required to be registered with the local police. Perhaps this was done here, too. Or, perhaps he had a telephone. Hadn't she read that most people in the United States had one in their homes?

Susanna rolled her head to the side and eyed the dirt-smudged, dull black contraption on the bedside table. Surely, if they could place a telephone in a reasonably priced hotel room such as this, an obviously well-off man like Jeffrey Kent could afford to have one. Her gaze shifted to the shelf below, where a dog-eared yellow and white directory lay. Without further deliberation, she reached for it and rolled into a sitting position.

Kent. She flipped the pages to the 'K's' and ran her finger down the columns. There were a lot of Kents, but not a Jeffrey or a Jeff, though there were several Kents prefaced with the initial *J*—J.A., J.N. and J.R. It wouldn't take long to call each of these.

Lifting the receiver, Susanna followed the printed instructions and dialed 9. When she heard the tone, she began to dial the first few digits of the first number. And slammed down the receiver.

What was she doing? she demanded. This was wrong. The man had already done far more than anyone in her country would have done in the name of courtesy and good manners. She had no right to impose on him further. No right at all.

Besides, she had gotten herself this far, so surely she'd be able to see this thing through without further inconveniencing a stranger?

She was on her own. Swallowing, she tilted her face toward the cracked and dusty ceiling she had come to know so well last night. She was alone, but then, when had she not been, one way or another, for most of her life? With her mother dead, Thomas Jaeger, for all that she bore his name and had shared his home, had rarely done more than treat her as part of the furniture.

Feeling stiff and brittle as if she were indeed made of wood, Susanna got off the bed. Traffic noises, notably absent until now, here at the edge of what last night's good Samaritan had called "downtown," could be heard above the steady drumming of rain up on the roof. It was a new day, and she would face it as she had faced each day that had gone before in the thirty years of her life: with optimism and the conviction that things could only get better.

Listen, she told herself, finding her way to the tiny bathroom adjoining her room. When have you ever had your very own bathroom before? Hmm? Never, that's when. Not to mention a shower, and towels that, though thin and slightly abrasive, at least weren't frayed and torn. So enjoy it, Susanna. For as long as you can.

Stripping off the rumpled skirt of her shabby gray suit, along with her plain white cotton blouse and underwear, Susanna fiddled with the shower faucets until she had them figured out, then stepped beneath the spray.

Hot running water! Heaven!

"The police station? Let's see, three blocks down, then left a block and a half should take you there."

"Thank you." Squinting against the rain, Susanna took her bearings along the woman's pointing finger. Adding a pleasant, "Have a nice day," the way everyone in this city seemed to do, she set out.

The sidewalks were crowded with people in a hurry. Used to it from years of living in a major metropolis, Susanna deftly dodged dripping umbrellas and jostling shoulders as she took in the sights. Her raincoat had long since stopped offering protection. Chilly moisture was seeping through the sweater and slacks she wore beneath it and into her bones. But now that she had a goal, a purpose, Susanna refused to let a little physical discomfort dampen her spirits.

She looked around with interest, noting that even though it was barely mid-November, Christmas already figured prominently in the window displays she was passing. She was awed by the wealth of available merchandise, nearly blinded by the glitz and glitter, and reminded by the manifold smells of good food that she hadn't eaten anything since the meal on the airplane. Perhaps a cup of coffee...

Susanna resolutely brushed the thought aside and crossed the street. She could not afford to indulge herself; she would eat at noon as planned. With luck, she would have something to celebrate by then.

The police station was in a large building of drab and discolored red bricks that was made even more depressing by the gloom of the day. Susanna combed back her sodden mess of corkscrew curls with not quite steady fingers, took a deep breath and entered. It had been her experience that dealing with officialdom was fraught with pitfalls, but last night the officer in the car had assured her that in this country the police were there to help. Besides, at this point, whom else did she have to turn to?

Inside the building it was warm, but the combination of damp clothing, unwashed bodies and the musty, dusty smell of bureaucracies everywhere made the warmth almost oppressive.

"Excuse me." Taking a deep breath, Susanna addressed the uniformed officer at the counter. "With whom do I speak about a...a missing person?"

"Missing for how long?"

"Well, I'm not sure." Susanna nervously licked her parched lips and tried to convince herself that the elderly officer really was as kindhearted as he appeared. There was nothing to be nervous about, she told herself. She had not done anything; her papers were in order. "I came to see a man, you see, at the address on this envelope, only to find him gone."

The officer took the envelope, glanced at the address, and handed it back with a shrug. "People move."

"Yes, but where?"

"Anywhere they want." Though not unfriendly, the officer's tone was dismissive. He shuffled some papers.

"His name is Joseph Harrison Miller."

"Miller's a dime-a-dozen name, miss. Unless your guy has a record...." Another shrug.

"But there must be something..." Desperate, Susanna clutched the counter. "Could you perhaps check? Your files, I mean?"

"Look, miss." The officer slammed a drawer. "I'm very busy. We're understaffed and underbudgeted. Unless there's been a crime, or you have a complaint, I'm afraid I can't—"

"What about Jeffrey Kent?" Susanna knew she was clutching at straws, but what else was there to cling to when all her hopes were being rapidly swept down the drain?

"That an alias?"

"Pardon? Oh. No, no, it's someone else. Another man."

"He missing, too?"

"No." Susanna didn't have to see the officer take up his pen and start to write to know he had lost interest in the conversation. "Thank you for your trouble," she mumbled to the top of his bent and balding head.

"You looking for Jeff Kent?" someone, a man, asked from behind her.

"Yes." Susanna turned on a surge of hope and found herself eye-to-eye with a cold, half-smoked cigar. It was clamped between the teeth of a tough-looking individual whose face, shock of red hair and clothes all looked equally rumpled. "Do you know him?"

"I do." The man looked her up and down. "You a friend of his?"

"No." He arched pale brows and she elaborated. "We met on the flight from Frankfurt yesterday."

"Ah. Back in town, is he?" A twist of the lips slid the cigar into the other corner of his mouth. Another sharp look assessed Susanna. "He take something of yours off the plane with him?"

"No, I—"

"You got something of his?"

"No. I—" This was not the time for her empty stomach to act up, Susanna thought on a wave of dizziness. She swallowed, forcing down the nausea. "I'm sorry, could I sit down?"

"In my office." She let herself be propelled past rows of cluttered desks into a cubicle at the back of the room. Knees aquiver, she sank onto a straight chair.

"Have some water."

"Thank you." Though she knew sweat beaded her brow, she felt cold. Perhaps she should have eaten, after all. The water helped. "You're very kind."

"Yeah, well." Voice gruff, expression stern, the man she now knew to be a police officer sat down behind his desk. He held a match to his cigar and puffed to get it started. "What's this all about?"

Briefly, Susanna told him. He fingered the letter she handed him. "The postmark is thirty years old. Hell—" he tossed it back "—the guy could be dead."

Susanna shook her head. Not because she knew better, but because all along she had refused to entertain that particular possibility with a single-minded consistency. She had staked years of her life on the conviction that Joseph Harrison Miller was still alive.

"And the name was what? Miller?"

"Yes."

"And he knew your mother in East Germany?"

"Yes."

"Miller. Joseph Harrison. Hmm." His brows collided in a fierce frown. "Something about that name..." The cigar wiggled as he talked. Ashes fell unheeded onto the desk. Muttering to himself, he reached for the phone and punched some numbers.

Bewildered, Susanna watched him, then snapped to attention when he said, "Kent? What the hell d'you mean who's this? It's Barn—Barney Golding—and don't give me that crap about waking you up. It's the middle of the day, so get those lazy bones of yours out of bed and get on over here...."

Funny, Jeff could have sworn he had put his diverting seatmate completely out of his mind, but the moment the phone rang to wake him, she had been the one he'd thought of. Susanna Jaeger.

Striding up the familiar police station stairs—before signing on with AP, he'd worked the court beat for *The Seattle Times* for several years—he wondered yet again what in hell she was doing in Barney Golding's office. She should be celebrating a long overdue reunion—or first meeting—with her father. Barely acknowledging the smattering of "Hey, Jeff"'s that greeted him, he headed straight for Barney's pitiful excuse for an office: two partitions, glassed at the top, enclosing a corner.

He entered without knocking, and his eyes immediately homed in on Susanna. She looked pale, wet and bedraggled. Dark circles beneath her eyes made them appear still darker and larger than they were naturally. The small smile she ventured when their gazes met quivered at the edges.

Keeping his eyes on hers, Jeff addressed Barney. "So what's going on, Barn?" Then, briefly pressing Susanna's shoulder, he asked her, "You okay?"

Susanna felt her smile widen as she looked at Jeff. How good it was, she thought, to see a familiar face. She nodded, said "I'm fine," then looked away, overcome by a rush of relief that threatened to bring more moisture to her eyes.

Jeff cupped her chin, raising it. "What happened?"

She blinked. "He, ah, he wasn't there...any longer."

"The letter she went by is thirty years old," Barney added. "Who the hell lives thirty years at the same address?"

"In Europe—" Susanna began to explain, but Golding cut her off.

"This is America, Miss Jaeger. We're a very mobile society." He scowled. "Frankly, it would've behooved you to establish contact with your Mr. Miller *before* you launched yourself on this wild-goose chase. Not that it would've done you any good."

"Goose chase? I don't understand."

"Ease up, Barn, will you?" Jeff said sharply. Susanna's bewilderment and vulnerability struck a protective chord he couldn't help but respond to. Right now, she was looking as lost as the scores of refugee children he had seen the world over. Casualties of events and circumstances beyond their control, they were all too often callously shuffled from place to place by some unfeeling authority. "Retrospective good advice solves nothing here."

"Neither does a collective bellyaching session, so cut me some slack." Golding chomped on his cigar. "I got work to do, so let's get on with this."

Jeff dragged a chair next to Susanna's. "With what, exactly? Why'd you bring her in?"

"We didn't. She came. In case you're interested, while we've been waiting for you, I've been doing some checking." Barney flipped through a file, took out a sheet of paper and handed it to Jeff. "Remember that one? Before your time working in the media, o'course, but it got megacoverage all over the place and you might've seen it."

Frowning, Jeff scanned the page. "Yeah. Harry Miller. Exchange of political prisoners at Checkpoint Charlie. I do seem to remember reading about it as part of some class or other in college." He looked up, knitting his brows, and handed back the paper. "But what's it got to do with this?" He jerked his head. "With her?"

"Miller's the guy the lady's looking for."

Jeff responded with a toneless whistle through his teeth. He locked gazes with Barney and contemplated him in a meaningful, thoughtful silence, wondering how to handle the matter.

Susanna, at the end of her tether, finally came unraveled. "I believe I'm the one whom this concerns!" she exclaimed, gripping Jeff's arm and jerking him to face her. "So kindly don't act as though I were not in the room." Her eyes burned into his. "What is the matter with my father? What's wrong?"

Jeff tossed Barney a questioning glance that was met with an open-palmed shrug. "That's why I called you in," Golding said. "She said she knew you. I figured I'd let you handle it."

"Gee, thanks," Jeff muttered, at a loss. How could he break to Susanna the fact that, to all intents and purposes, Joseph Harrison Miller was dead? That there was nothing she could do here, so she might just as well get on the next plane and go back to where she'd come from?

Somehow the thought of that depressed him.

"Handle what?" Susanna said when Jeff only stared at her in silence. The look in his eyes reinforced the terrible feeling that the few remaining shreds of her dream were about to be destroyed. Her earlier nausea returned with a vengeance. The room spun. Cold sweat popped out all over her body.

"Oh, please," she whispered, feeling herself toppling off the chair. She reached out, but her hands only touched air. "Excuse me, but I think... I'm going to be sick...."

Everything that followed became part of the jumbled dream in which Susanna was pursued by men in uniform. She awoke to find herself in a bed. The ceiling above this one was white and clean, bordered by pink and blue stripes. In short, it was nothing like the ceiling she had stared at the previous night.

This was not her hotel.

The thought ought to have alarmed her, she knew, but it didn't. Nor did the realization that someone had stripped off her clothes and stuffed her into a voluminous flannel nightgown. Jeffrey Kent? She neither knew nor, in her present frame of mind, cared. She did vaguely recall being carried out of and into places by him, and a kindly female voice tut-tutting over her. His wife? That, too, Susanna did not know. She had been too drained to react to any of it then, and still was.

It didn't matter. Nothing mattered now that she knew all of her plans had gone hopelessly awry. Her dream had been shattered. She groped for the locket. It had slipped around to the side and lay on the pillow next to her throat. But this time, touching it gave her no comfort.

She must have slept some more, because the next thing she knew it was dark outside the curtained window. It was quiet, too; no rain beat against the panes any longer, nor was there that eerily howling wind. Good smells—food smells—were wafting into the room. Its door was ajar, and through the opening a smiling face peered in at her.

"You're awake, I see." A rotund little woman bustled in. "Wonderful." She took Susanna's hand and patted it. "Are you feeling better, my dear? Are you hungry?"

A very noisy growl from her stomach had Susanna furiously blushing, and made the other woman laugh with delight. "Excellent! Dinner is ready in just a few minutes. We were hoping you'd be able to join us."

Overwhelmed, Susanna struggled to sit up. "I'm sorry," she murmured, looking around and seeing nothing familiar, not even her clothes. "Where . . . ?"

"Why, how thoughtless of me!" the woman exclaimed softly. She reached out and stroked a hand over Susanna's tousled hair in a gesture that was achingly reminiscent of her own mother's touch. "Jeff told me, poor dear. So much has happened. You're wondering who I am and where you are. I'm Elaine Kent, Susanna. Jeffrey's mother. And this is his sister Joanne's room. She's married. So now it's really a guest room." She leaned forward and gave Susanna a quick, reassuring hug. "We're delighted to have you as our guest, my dear."

"But . . ." Susanna met Jeff's mother's sympathetic gaze through a curtain of tears she could no longer stem. In the face of so much kindness, her emotions were completely adrift.

Elaine Kent's tone firmed. "No buts, my dear. You're more than welcome to stay until Jeff can work things out for you. Meanwhile—" she bustled over to a closet and opened it "—I believe you'll find something to wear in here. And the bathroom is through there." She pointed to a door while walking toward the one through which she had entered. "Go ahead and freshen up and then follow your nose downstairs. All right?"

Not waiting for a reply—not that Susanna felt capable of making one—she left.

Her thoughts a riot of confusion, Susanna stared at the now closed door. Jeff. Jeff's home. Until Jeff works things out, his mother had said. *Gott im Himmel!*

She scrambled off the bed, searched vainly for her own clothes, then collapsed, covering her face with her hands. What was happening to her? How had she ended up in the home of strangers, an object of charity and pity? She had taken such care to plot out the course she wanted her life to take!

Let Jeffrey Kent work things out? What could he do that she could not do for herself? And what had he been about to tell her about her father?

The need to know was what brought her to her feet again. The same need had her slip into a pair of jeans and a sweatshirt that weren't hers after tidying her hair with someone else's brush and comb.

Voices, as well as the wonderful aroma of roasting meat, guided her hesitant feet into a bright, cheery kitchen. Three pairs of eyes, in varying shades of green and blue, swung toward her. Without exception, their expression held welcome. Susanna had never experienced anything like it.

"Excuse me . . ." Helpless, her gaze sought Jeff's.

"Susanna." He was instantly by her side. "Come on in." Placing an arm around her shoulders, he guided her all the way into the room. "You've met Mom over there," he said, loving his mother for the warm smile she gave Susanna. He could feel the nervous tension in the rigid set of her shoulders. An awful lot of surprises had come at this woman, none of them pleasant. The one yet to come, the one he had in store for her, might well prove to be the last straw.

So he would tell her after dinner. Things always looked better on a full stomach.

He led her toward the table, saying, "And this is my father, Ronald Kent."

The older man rose, pulling out a chair for Susanna as he did so. "A pleasure to see you up and about, Susanna. Have a seat."

"Dad's a man of few words," Jeff confided into her ear.

"I hope you don't mind, my dear." Jeff's mother was already putting bowls of food upon the table. "Eating family style here in the kitchen, I mean."

Mind? Susanna thought it all quite extraordinary. This kitchen, all white painted wood and stainless steel, to her was like something out of a fantasy. And yet, for all its sleek efficiency, the room had a coziness that invited a person to linger.

Jeff had seated himself across from her, with his father on her left and his mother on her right. "Well," said Elaine, cheeks aglow from her labors at the stove as she cast an approving glance around the table. "It's like old times, Jeffrey, when both you and your sister were home."

Not quite, Jeff thought while smiling agreement. The woman across from him might be in his sister's clothes and chair, but she was definitely *not* his sister. His sister had never drawn his gaze as this woman did, nor made him want to touch....

"I hope you're feeling better," he said, forcing his thoughts back into approved channels. "You gave me quite a turn—a fright," he explained, recognizing the bemused frown as the one Susanna wore when sifting through her stock of colloquialisms, "in Barney's office this morning."

"Oh. I'm so sorry about that." Susanna carefully took one pork chop and passed the platter to Jeff's father. "It was all . . . too much, suddenly . . ."

"Of course it was," Elaine sympathized, though Jeff had only cursorily filled her in. "You poor thing. Try some of the broccoli, dear. Don't scowl, Jeffrey, broccoli's good for you. Ron, please pass Susanna the gravy. Eat, dear. Eat. You'll feel better. . . ."

Under Elaine Kent's watchful eye, Susanna ate. Three helpings, and only a belated sense of decorum kept her from taking a fourth. When Elaine brought out dessert, however, she was glad she had restrained herself.

"So this is apple pie," she said, savoring each flaky bite topped by vanilla ice cream. She smiled at her hostess. "Your son was saving his appetite for this on the airplane."

"He was?" Elaine beamed. "It's always been his favorite. Another piece, Jeffy?"

But Jeff declined. Truth to tell, it hadn't just been the broccoli he'd had to force down. The prospect of having to deliver the final blow to Susanna after dinner had stolen his appetite.

The meal over, Susanna expressed her thanks. "If you'd just tell me where to find my own clothes," she added, "I'll change and take a taxi back to my hotel. You've all been most kind."

"Why, not a bit," Elaine protested. "We're happy to help." She looked at her son. "Jeffrey, tell her."

"In a while, Mom." His parents had offered to have Susanna stay with them for as long as she was in the country. Jeff's sister Joanne had been an exchange student in Germany, and she'd been treated like one of the family there. This, the Kents felt, was their chance to reciprocate.

"Why don't I drive you?" Jeff suggested to Susanna, figuring they would talk en route. Afterward he would bring her back here. "As to your clothes, they were drenched. Wet from the rain," he elaborated. "I took the liberty of sending them to the cleaners. You'll have them back tomorrow."

"Oh," Susanna murmured, acutely uncomfortable with the way control of her life and belongings seemed to have slipped from her grasp. She was used to relying only on herself. "Th-thank you."

Heading downtown, Jeffrey was still casting around for an appropriate opening to the news he had to give her when Susanna broke the silence that had grown a little charged.

"So, ah, about Joseph Miller—my father. Is he dead?"

Jeff decided not to pull any punches. "To you, yes."

"To me?" Shocked, Susanna turned sharply. "What does that mean? To me?"

Jeff negotiated a turn and, after a glance into the rearview mirror, eased over one lane. "It means that he's inaccessible to you, Susanna. Or to anyone else from his past."

Susanna frowned. "I don't understand. Is he alive then?"

"He's alive."

"But I cannot see him?"

"No."

"But why?" She leaned toward him, her tone urgent. "I *have* to see him, Jeffrey, or else I won't be allowed to stay in this country." Desperation had her clutching his arm again. "What have they done to him? Tell me. Why can't I see him? Please, Jeffrey, if you know, you must tell me."

"All right." Jeff pulled the car to the curb and cut the engine. He turned to face her. "Some twenty-odd years ago your father's life was in jeopardy. He'd been working for the U.S. government and—"

He looked into her eyes, saw the despair and closed his own. "The fact, Susanna, is that Joseph Harrison Miller is no longer . . . Joseph Harrison Miller."

3521 Harborview St.
Seattle, Wash.
29 April

My sweet little mother,

A girl? I couldn't be happier. No, strike that. Of course I could. I would be happier if we were together, if we were a family in the way I believe we were meant to be....

There's a lot of trouble here. I only live for the day when you and our child will be able to come to me. Meanwhile, my heart and I are in this locket I send to you. I love you....

Ever yours,
Harry

P.S. I have been sent to Seattle. Please note the new address....

Chapter Three

"What?" Eyes round, Susanna stared at Jeff. "What are you saying? What do you mean, he's no longer...?" She blinked, looking at the fists she'd formed and shaking her head, probably as much in denial as incomprehension. "How can he not be...?" Frustrated, she raised her eyes to Jeff's. "Can you please explain to me how somebody suddenly becomes somebody else?"

"People change all the time," Jeff told her quietly. The feelings he saw in her eyes—utter bewilderment, disillusionment and pain—clutched at his heart. "In

Harry Miller's case it was a bit more than that, however,'' he went on. After another short pause, he asked, "Just how much do you know about your father, Susanna?"

She frowned. "Know about him?"

"Yeah. About what he did. Why he spent so much time in your country. How he met your mother, that sort of thing."

Susanna shrugged, looking down again. "Not much. His letters don't explain, and there was no contact at all after the third one. Mother would talk to me about him, of course. She very much loved him, I think. She said they'd met through her work. She was a translator for one of the government ministries."

"Ahh."

His intonation made Susanna glance at him sharply. "That is significant?"

"Possibly." Jeff turned face front again. Staring at the nearly deserted street, he briefly debated whether to tell her more, not that he knew that much, himself. Miller had figured prominently in some deals the U.S. government had made with the Soviets a couple of decades ago. Most of it had been classified, of course, but what little they'd found out, the press had played up. Some guy by the name of Otrovsky—a Soviet— had been involved. There'd been trouble of some sort, but Jeff was vague as to its nature....

Deciding she was entitled to the full truth—if she didn't know it already—he said, "Harry Miller was a spy, Susanna."

Her gasp told him she hadn't known. That pleased him somehow. Whatever dirty dealings there might have been, they had not touched her. Possibly that could be a plus for her—in the event he could convince Barney Golding and ultimately the Feds to give her something to go on.

Mentally figuring the angles, Jeff draped both arms over the steering wheel, resting his chin on top. "About eighteen years ago it became expedient that he disappear," he told Susanna. "The Feds spirited him away and gave him a new identity. These days nobody knows where he is or who he is. Or if they do, they're not talking."

Silence; followed at length by a shaky little laugh. "Well," said Susanna, hearing her voice roughened by an ache in her throat that would not let itself be swallowed. How ironic, she thought, struggling with hysteria.

Thomas Jaeger's last, bitter words to his stepdaughter had been, "I have raised you as my own, yet you would sell your soul to be a daughter to that *imperialist*. Just as at one time your mother would have sold hers to be his wife. But she died here, in this country, and without him. And so will you, Susanna. So will you."

Ever since then, Susanna had resolved to prove him wrong. Thomas Jaeger had married Maria when Susanna had been only two years old and had been as good a father to her as he'd been able, but he'd been a cold man, as well as very much a communist. And while he had undoubtedly loved Susanna's mother, the knowledge that Maria had once given herself, her heart and her trust to an American had tinged that love with ugly hues of bitterness and resentment.

After his death, Susanna had scrimped and saved

and worked all the more to make Maria's dream, and her own, come true and get away.

And she had done it—almost. Now she was here. Here in America. Only to find—

"No, damn it!"

Jeffrey's startled reaction told her she had spoken the words aloud. Since they succinctly summed up what she felt, Susanna didn't apologize. Instead, she looked Jeff in the eye with grim determination. "It cannot end here," she said, "I won't let it. I *will* find him—"

"How?" Jeff asked gently. "Susanna." He took her hand. "You don't even know the man's name."

"Then I'll find it out. I'll go to the authorities—"

"They won't help you. They can't."

"*Somebody* can. Your friend, Detective Golding." Susanna was grasping at straws and knew it, but to just accept, to just give up—no. No, no, *no*. "Surely he can—?"

"He can't, Susanna." Because he couldn't bear just to sit helplessly in the face of Susanna's desperation, Jeff started the car and eased into the traffic. "And even if he could—"

"*Aha!*" Susanna exclaimed. "So there is a possibility."

"There are always possibilities. The question is, how practical are they? As I started to say—even if he could, there's a time factor to consider. How long's your visa good for?"

"Six weeks. Why?"

"Why? Because your chances of anything being resolved in that short a time are practically nil."

"Practically. That means there is a chance."

Jeff shook his head; he opened his mouth to object, but Susanna cut him off.

"No, Jeffrey. I must at least try. For as long as I have here, I must make the effort. I have nothing to give but time, and I have nothing at all to lose. You see, I promised...." Her hand flew to her throat and touched the golden heart. "I promised my mother that one day, somehow, I would go to him. And go to him I will."

"Susanna—"

"No. Don't try to dissuade me, Jeffrey. I haven't gotten as far as this by giving up, and I won't give up now." She cast him a glance, took in his frown, and placed one hand on his arm. "Please don't worry. I won't be hanging on your coattails. You've been more than kind, but I'll get on on my own after this."

"Like hell you will."

Jeff had just gotten a look at the Miranda Court Hotel.

Having always been in charge—first of herself then, after her mother became ill, of the entire Jaeger household—Susanna was not at all sure she liked the willy-nilly manner in which Jeffrey Kent was taking over her life.

He had checked her out of the hotel in blatant disregard of her feelings on the matter. Next, he had installed her in his parents' home in spite of her protests, and *then* he had proceeded to set up a meeting with Barney Golding—a meeting that would not include her.

"Look," she said to him, pacing a track into the Kent's plush wall-to-wall carpet. "I appreciate all you've done, but I'm really very uncomfortable imposing—''

"You're not imposing." Jeff crossed his legs and watched her pace. She moved very well, he noted. *Very* well. Joanne's jeans and pale pink sweater accomplished what Susanna's wardrobe of drab grays never could—they made her look delectably female. Too damn delectable for his peace of mind.

"I'm accustomed of taking care of myself," Susanna persisted, counting twenty paces from the grandfather clock to the window and thinking that American rooms certainly were spacious. "And I believe I am within my rights when I say I should be in on that meeting."

"Your rights have nothing to do with it." Too restless to sit, Jeff went to join her at the window. "It's a preliminary meeting. All I'm going to do is run the request past him and see what the reaction is. And that's best done one-on-one."

He noted absently that it was raining again. He didn't mind. Fact was, he had missed the stuff something awful during his time in the desert. Hell, for the first time ever during this last stint, he had actually missed home. He'd been homesick, and it had hurt.

Susanna had no home to be homesick for, but she longed to change that. Jeff realized how very painful it must be to want something so much, to finally have it within reach, and then to have it snatched away again. She was trying to find her father; she was trying to find a home to which, in Jeff's opinion, she was entitled. And that was why he'd made the decision to do what he could to help her.

"Does it rain much in...what was the name of your hometown again?" he asked, after the silence between them had lasted a while.

"Linzberg. And no, it doesn't rain there as much as it seems to do here."

"D'you have Thanksgiving in your country?"

The non sequitur earned him a startled frown. He responded to it with a small smile. "Humor me. I'm trying to get so we're no longer strangers. Maybe then you'll relax about staying in this house."

At that her lips curved, too. "We have a saying," she said, folding her arms, "something to the effect that houseguests of any sort are like fish. After three days they smell bad."

"The word is 'stink.'"

She shrugged. "Whatever. I don't intend to turn into a fish."

"No danger of that when you've only been here one day. And you haven't answered my question."

"About Thanksgiving? Yes, we have it. In October, I believe."

"You believe? Don't you know?"

"Of course I know. It's in October. *Erntedankfest.* But it's not as if it were a, you know, a large deal."

"Big," Jeff corrected automatically, adding, "And it certainly is a big deal in this country. Turkey Day, next week Thursday."

"Turkey Day?" Susanna queried. "You call a holiday the purpose of which is for the farmers to give thanks for good, er...? What do you call it—bringing in the grains and things from the fields?"

"Harvest?"

"Yes, thank you. That's it. *Erntedankfest* means thanks for harvest. So why do you call it turkey day?"

Enchanted by Susanna's studious expression and unceasing desire to know and understand all things American, Jeff laughed. "Why'nt you stick around, Miss Jaeger, and find out? You'll be in for a treat, I promise you."

The look she gave him was bittersweet. "Just being here is a treat, Mr. Kent. But, surely, by next Thursday I'll be elsewhere, no?"

"I..." *hope not,* Jeff found himself wanting to say as his gaze dipped into hers and caught the dreamy longing there. "...really can't say," he amended, adding, "but if not, we'd very much like you to stay for the feast."

She swallowed visibly, her smile quivering. "Are all Americans as generous and kind as you are?"

What a question. Discomfited, Jeff would have liked to look away, but found himself lost in the velvet darkness of her eyes. Was it really generosity and kindness that motivated his actions with regard to this comely foreigner? On the part of his parents, certainly. But on his?

Their gazes lingered. As the moment lengthened and the silence grew heavy, something arced between them. Something Susanna responded to. Her eyes, rounding, grew darker still and as luminous as black diamonds.

Jeff saw awareness take hold, and a corresponding flutter of attraction tensed every nerve in his body. Disconcerted by the emotions he saw in her and felt in himself, he blinked and looked away.

Feeling suddenly out of his depth, he fumbled his glasses off his nose and, rubbing a hand across his face, expelled the air that somehow seemed to have gotten trapped in his chest. He shot Susanna a quick glance. She was staring at the carpet, brow furrowed, lips compressed. She looked every bit as self-conscious as he felt.

Hell of a note, he thought, to be catching himself attracted to this woman. No way could it lead to anything; they had a mission of sorts to accomplish, but once that was done, so would they be. Meanwhile, no complications were wanted.

Deciding that, for the moment, retreat seemed the best course of action, Jeff stuck his glasses back on his face. He started to touch Susanna's shoulder, thought better of it and moved away. "I, er, I'll see you later, all right?"

He was out of the room before she looked up.

Troubled by the feelings that had briefly flared between them, Susanna slowly turned back to the window. Across the street, rain-slickered children were wading through puddles.

Two little girls, perhaps a year apart in age. One dark, one with coppery curls much like Jeffrey Kent's...

Abruptly she turned away.

"Why, my dear, how sad you look." Elaine Kent had come into the room. Hands outstretched, her expression concerned, she came to Susanna. "Is there anything I can do? I met Jeffrey in the hall—did he upset you?"

"No." With an effort, Susanna summoned a smile. "I was just...thinking."

Elaine tut-tutted. "A bad habit, I'm told, and one I avoid as much as possible." Humor brightened her eyes, crinkling them at the corners. "Want to know what I do when I feel a bout of thinking coming on? I go shopping."

Linking her arm with Susanna's, she pulled her along. "Come, child, let me introduce you to the American mall. I'm sure you'll find the place a most wonderful diversion."

"How about we go to a movie?" Jeff proposed to the table at large over dinner that night. "A film," he elaborated automatically for Susanna's benefit, responding to her quick smile of acknowledgment with a crooked one of his own.

"Why not just rent a video?" his mother countered. "One outing a day's about all I'm up to these days. That mall was a zoo."

"Really crowded," Jeff said to Susanna.

"I know." Her cheeks dimpled. "I was there."

"You were, huh?" Jeff hadn't realized she'd gone along with his mother. He'd spent the afternoon trying to connect with some old girlfriends in an effort to get Susanna Jaeger out of his head. He hadn't been very successful on either count. "So what did you think?"

Susanna exchanged a quick, twinkling glance with Elaine, then made everyone laugh by taking her head in both hands, rolling her eyes and saying, "Like *wow*, man! Too much!"

"Buy anything?" Jeff asked, stirring sugar into his coffee and pushing the bowl to Susanna.

"Oh, no. There's really nothing I need. I—"

"She insisted on buying *me* the cutest little figurine," Elaine cut in with mock severity, "even though I expressly forbade it."

Susanna colored. "It was nothing. Just a token—"

"It most certainly is something," contradicted Elaine, rising to fetch a small porcelain figure from her housekeeping desk by the window. "See? It's the darlingest little nurse...."

"Nurse, huh?" Jeff duly admired the figure before fixing his gaze upon the decidedly discomfited Susanna. "Any significance?"

She shrugged. "It's what I am, you see. What I have been for the past twelve years...."

"Twelve years?" Jeff's brows arched. "Now I *know* they train nurses differently in other countries, but even so..." He made a show of calculating. "Twelve years'd make you at least—"

"Thirty," Susanna admitted quite freely. "After the required nine years of *Grundschule*—that is, basic general education—I was fifteen, and I began my nurse's apprenticeship. That means three years of a combination of practical and theoretical training. I was finished at eighteen, except for ongoing specializing courses I enrolled in from time to time in order to, you know, move forward—"

"Advance."

"Yes." Susanna nodded. "To advance in my career."

"But how fascinating!" Elaine exclaimed. "Isn't it, Ron?"

Jeff's father nodded, apparently content to be a passive participant in the conversation.

"I toyed with the notion of going into nursing my-self once upon a time," Elaine went on. "But in this country nursing schools are generally part of a uni-versity, and before I could enroll, dear Ronald here..."

"Ran her to ground and married her," Jeff con-cluded wryly as his mother gave a girlish giggle and coy glance at her quietly smiling husband, and left the sentence dangling.

"We eloped," said Elaine, reminiscently.

"They ran away together," Jeff translated with a wink for Susanna, downplaying the pride he took in his parents' obvious delight with the story and each other.

"I think that's lovely," Susanna said softly, blink-ing against the sudden sting of tears. "My mother and father—Harry Miller—had a love like that, too," she added. "How wonderful it would have been if—"

She broke off, becoming aware that the three Kents were looking at her sympathetically, and afraid she might have grown maudlin. "I'm sorry."

"Don't." Jeff laid a hand over hers and kept it there in spite of the jolt he received from the contact of skin on skin. "It'll all work out, Susanna. You'll see. Now," he added with deliberate forcefulness after a pause and getting to his feet. "I suggest you and I go see a movie and leave those two old lovebirds to do the dishes...."

The film they saw was a Western of sorts. In turn humorous and poignant, it was the story of three men, friends, seeking escape and adventure on a staged cattle drive and finding all of that—and themselves, too—in the process.

Susanna sat entranced throughout, laughing like a kid at the funny parts, biting her lips when things turned tender or sad.

Jeff had insisted on buying her popcorn, causing a response of, "But why?"

"Because," he'd explained, shoving the bag into one hand and a soft drink into the other, "that's how it's done."

"That's how *what* is done?"

"Moviegoing," he'd said. "It's the American way."

That had shut her up, as he'd known it would. But three-quarters of the way through the film she was still just holding the stuff. Unable to stand it any longer, Jeff brought his mouth to her ear.

"Want me to hold your drink?" he whispered, his voice roughening a little in response to her closeness; the scent of her enfolded him warmly and sweetly.

She only shook her head, a movement that had silky tendrils of hair caressing his lips. Jeff took a deep breath and swallowed.

"But you're not eating," he said.

"Shh..." She turned her head, frowned at him, and their noses touched. Their lips almost did the same. Almost. Something like shock froze them—nose to nose, mouth to mouth, for one slow, thunderous heartbeat.

Jeff drew back, and in the same instant Susanna snapped her head away to face forward.

Both stared at the screen then as if completely absorbed in the action there, but in truth neither grasped, or was aware of, anything beyond their nearness and reaction to each other.

That's twice, Jeffrey thought, sweating and fighting the urge to loosen a suddenly constricting collar when what he was wearing was a turtleneck. Third time's the charm?

Three days later. Saturday. Susanna and Jeff were once again in the living room. Alone. Jeff was on the phone.

"Thanks, Barn," he was saying. "You bet. First thing tomorrow. I owe you one, bud."

Jeff broke the connection and slowly turned toward Susanna, who stood, eyes wide with apprehension, hands tightly clasped and pressed against her mouth.

Unable to stifle a grin, he gave her a nod and a thumbs-up signal.

She gasped. "They've found him?"

"Well...let's just say they've admitted they know where he is."

"But that's good." Susanna sounded unsure.

"It's a start."

"Yes! Oh, Jeffrey!" With a whoop, Susanna threw her arms wide and flung them around his neck.

Caught off guard and thrown off balance, Jeff found his arms closing around her reflexively.

"Thank you, thank you, thank you," Susanna was mumbling against his throat, and all Jeff could think was that it felt as good to hold her as he'd known it would. When she raised her head to smile mistily up at him, however, his brain cut out completely.

He kissed her.

And immediately wished he hadn't, because the moment their lips touched, he knew several things. He knew this was not going to be a simple, quick, "thanks-and-you're-welcome" kind of kiss. He knew that this kiss alone could never sate the hunger it had aroused. And he knew with an aching certainty that what he wanted, perhaps even *needed* from Susanna Jaeger was more than just a kiss; what he wanted to give her was more than just fleeting friendship and a helping hand.

Susanna had never known male lips could be so soft. And they weren't for long. Soon they hardened. Soon they gripped hers instead of pressing gently. Soon they demanded passion instead of merely giving affection.

In response, just for an instant, she gave him both. She opened her mouth for his tongue, settled her body where his hands urged she should and reveled in his touch.

As Jeff felt her relax and respond, he widened his stance and welcomed her hips into the cradle of his. He kissed her more deeply, touched her more fully, and because he wanted still more, he forced himself to stop, just as Susanna was beginning to move away from him. He let her go.

Susanna quickly backed up a step, afraid to stay close, yet oh, so tempted to do just that. She stared at Jeff and saw him staring at her with something like wonder, shock and not a little fear. She didn't pretend not to be shaken by what they had just shared.

Neither did Jeff, she realized. He removed his glasses without breaking eye contact. Susanna could see that his were bright, their pupils wide open. His nostrils flared as he inhaled sharply.

"I shouldn't have done that," he said, reaching out to touch a finger to her well-kissed lips. Apparently thinking better of it, he lowered his arm. "But I'll be damned if I'm sorry."

The words were like a precious gift, the implications caused Susanna's throat to close with emotions. Sweetness, affection, love—these qualities had been scarce, no, nonexistent for so long now that she had all but lost the capacity to deal with them.

Feeling her lower lip start to tremble, she tightly closed her mouth and tried for a smile. "Won't you . . . ?" She swallowed. "Won't you please tell me wh-what exactly Mr. Golding said?"

"He said the Feds agree yours are extraordinary circumstances." Jeff cleared his throat to get rid of a lingering trace of huskiness. He applauded her attempt to restore a semblance of normality between them and did his best to do the same. Replacing his glasses, he collected his thoughts. "They know where he is and they've decided to contact him. If he's amenable to talking with them—and it's strictly up to him, understand—they'll tell him you're in the country and wish to see him. They want something of yours that would convince him you are who you say you are—"

Susanna's hand flew to her throat. "The locket."

"If he's satisfied, and willing to see you—"

"But why would he not be?"

"Thirty years is a long time, Susanna. Harry Miller doesn't only have a different name, he's a different man with a different life. You're like a specter from the past. Not many people are comfortable with specters."

"But I'm his daughter, not a ghost."

"You're also, potentially, a threat to his safety, Susanna." Jeff came to her and tried to raise her chin, but upset by his words, she turned her face away. "We have a start, Susanna," he told her. "You were happy a moment ago and rightly so—we're on the right track and making progress. Smile," he said gently. "Things are looking up."

Suddenly, Susanna was afraid again, afraid that even now all manner of things could go wrong. She hugged herself on a shiver of trepidation, and lifted her eyes to Jeff's. "Will he want me, Jeffrey, do you think?"

Jeff didn't know. Frankly, he doubted it. But faced with the hope and the yearning in Susanna's Gypsy eyes, he didn't dare voice those doubts. He gently cupped her cheek, stroking it with his thumb.

"Silly woman," he murmured affectionately, slipping his hand into her hair to cradle the back of her head. "Who wouldn't want you?"

Chapter Four

Jeff told himself it was because he loved his country, his state, his hometown that he was willing to go out of his way to introduce Susanna Jaeger to as many things American as he could while they waited for word from her father. If this proved not to be a chore, well, that was a bonus. He was a man, she was a woman. There was chemistry between them, and while messing with it might well not be the wisest thing he'd ever done, it was exciting. Exhilarating.

No other kisses had followed that impulsive and revealing one of the day before. But the memory of it always seemed to be there between them, just below the surface, until a chance touch or intercepted glance would bring it pulsing to life.

Oh, yes, he thought, smoothing the hair back from his temples and giving himself a last, approving nod in the mirror before striding, whistling, out of his bachelor digs to his parents' house. Oh yes, indeed!

"Ready?" he asked, sticking only his head through the back door and seeing Susanna at the kitchen counter with his mother. She had her threadbare raincoat on and, at his question, turned toward him with her finger in her mouth.

Lucky finger, Jeff thought; their gazes met, and there it was again, awareness. It made his eyes burn, and turned Susanna's cheeks rosy.

"Your mother's making the most marvelous chocolate pudding," she mumbled, self-consciously wiping her finger on her coat after guiltily yanking it out of her mouth like a four-year-old thumb sucker caught in the act.

"Mousse," said Elaine, offering Jeff a sample on a teaspoon. "For after dinner tonight."

"Hmm. This *is* good, Mom." Jeff, his gaze still on Susanna, dropped a kiss upon his mother's cheek. "But I'm afraid Susanna and I won't be here for dinner. We're gonna play tourist at Seattle Center and maybe eat at the top of the Space Needle."

Catching Susanna's hand, he pulled her out the door. "Be sure and save us some, though."

"Everything is so large over here," Susanna marveled, craning her neck to see the tops of the high rises they passed driving down Fourth Avenue toward Seattle Center, the former Expo grounds turned amusement park. "Skyscrapers really *are* what these are."

"A little strangely put," Jeff observed, slanting her a grin. "But true."

"I imagined only New York and Chicago would be like this...."

"And that all you'd see out West would be cowboys and Indians?"

Susanna blushed. "Well, not quite really, but—"

"Almost?"

She caught the twinkle in his eye, laughed, and a little sheepishly conceded, "Yes."

"Disappointed?"

"Perhaps a little."

Time to look for a spot to park. As they approached Denny Way, Jeff recalled a lot not far from their destination and kept his eye out for an entrance.

"If we drive into the country I might be able to offer you a cowboy or two," he told Susanna with a chuckle. "But you're as liable to find an Indian in one of these *skyscrapers*, practicing law and wearing a three-piece Italian suit, as anywhere."

"Really?"

She sounded so disappointed, Jeff burst out laughing. "Sorry, sweetheart, but that's called progress...."

Susanna said no more, but suddenly looked so shaken, he swung toward her the moment the car was parked. "What's wrong?"

She was staring at him, eyes wide. "Why did you say that?"

"Say what?" She'd lost him. Jeff frowned. "About progress?"

"'Sweetheart,'" she whispered, her eyes softening with bittersweet emotions as she gazed fixedly into his. "You said to me *sweetheart*, Jeffrey, and I know that it's an endearment between ... between—lovers...."

Jeez! Jeff closed his eyes on a sharply inhaled breath. Susanna's sudden shyness and—for a woman of thirty—unmistakably genuine air of innocence completely disarmed and shook him.

A little shakily he let go of the air in his lungs.

"For heaven's sake, Susanna..." Then he opened his eyes to meet hers and, unable to say any more, simply gathered her close, saying in a husky whisper, "You do the craziest things to me."

She pressed her face to his, but kept her hands in her lap. "You do crazy things to me, too, Jeffrey."

He rubbed her back, his common sense struggling to outrace his rapidly accelerating pulse and galloping hormones. "If circumstances were different..."

"Y-yes..."

"If it were any other time and you were any other woman..."

Susanna stiffened.

Jeff drew back a little and caught her chin to make her look at him. "A less vulnerable woman, Susanna."

"Oh."

"I'd like nothing more than for you and me to be lovers, if that's how things were."

As his thumb stroked her cheek, her eyelids fluttered. Jeff felt her swallow against the heel of his hand touching her throat. Then she uttered a needy little sound and he was kissing her, kissing her with something close to desperation, fueled by the shocking certainty that this woman was somehow meant to be special to him. God help him, he couldn't bear the thought of letting her out of his life so soon. And so completely.

The passionate fire of Jeffrey's kisses was like a torch that set aflame the flimsy defenses Susanna had been struggling to erect, reducing them to a heap of ash that scattered like hot desert sand. The arm not trapped between the car seat and their straining bodies crept up to encircle Jeff's neck; she melted into him. Into the kiss. She savored the feel of him—hard male body, butter-soft leather jacket, the mixture of silk and crisp, bristly waves that was his hair. He smelled of soap, leather and man. Clean. So clean. He tasted of desire and . . . chocolate mousse.

She wanted him. All of him. For all time.

But because she knew he could never be hers in any way other than this—there was no time; their lives, their goals, their dreams didn't mesh—so she strove to put into her response all the longing for him she felt. But also all her gratitude, affection—and regret.

Her tongue welcomed his, danced and mated with his. Her free hand stroked, gripped, flexed and released like his. Her body, pulsing with need and separated from the ultimate closeness by layers of clothes, rubbed and strained against his. The car's window steamed up, creating for a moment a cocoon of illusory privacy. The harsh rap of knuckles against glass was a jarring intrusion.

"Go away," Jeffrey murmured, taking his time ending the kiss. His eyes were heavy-lidded and unfocused as he gazed into Susanna's equally slumberous ones and nibbled at the feast her passion-puffed lips offered him.

"Reality knocks," he quipped with a husky half groan, half chuckle that Susanna echoed. Once more he touched her lips, lingered, then drew away.

Another peppering of sharp-knuckled raps and a loud, "Hey, buddy, how 'bout neckin' on your own time?" dispersed the haze. Reluctantly they straightened. Loath to end the interlude, hands continued to touch, to smooth. They exchanged grins that went from hesitant to delightedly carefree in one heartbeat, and then, with a sigh, Jeff rolled down the window.

"What can I do for you?" he asked with all the poise and graciousness of a man answering a knock on the door of his home.

The all-set-to-be-irate parking lot attendant was visibly taken aback by Jeff's poise. "Uh..." he faltered, "um..." then appeared to recall his responsibilities and position. "Either you move the car, Mac, or you gimme fi' bucks. This here's no lovers' lane, you know...."

Dinner in the revolving restaurant at the top of the Space Needle was the crowning touch to what Susanna considered the most perfect night of her life to date. Her head abuzz with new impressions and her senses aquiver from Jeff's nearness and loverlike attentiveness, she was happier than she could ever remember being.

"Thank you," she said simply, pulling her gaze from the dazzling sight of Seattle and its skyscrapers dressed for the holidays. "I never dreamed it could be like this."

"The city?" Jeff teased to stem the rush of tenderness her joy never failed to bring to his heart. "The day?" He raised his glass. "The wine?"

"Everything. All of it. It's perfect." She set down her own glass untasted and bit her lips. Her gaze clouded. "It frightens me a little. It's too much—"

"Too much?"

"Do I deserve this?" she asked in whisper. "Is it right to be so happy when so many others—?"

"Susanna..." Jeff caught her hand. "Don't."

"I'm sorry." She inhaled shakily and tried for a smile of apology. "Am I being a wet sheet?"

"That's 'blanket.' And no, you're not." Jeff squeezed her hand and grew serious, too. "You're a caring, sensitive human being. That's why you feel as you do. And you know something? Most of us who are fortunate enough to call this country home share those feelings at one time or another."

"Really?"

"Yeah," Jeff said dryly. "Really. Oh, I know," he added, releasing her hand to lean back and gesture, "that isn't the popular perception of Americans in much of the international community—Yanks are brash, naive and self-indulgent, many people think— but it's true, nonetheless. We Americans know we're blessed with an embarrassment of riches and consequently there are plenty of times when we ask ourselves how we got so lucky. And we might feel a need to be apologetic at those times."

"Apologetic?" Susanna's tone was incredulous. "But why should you?"

Leaning forward again, Jeff reached for his wineglass and frowned at its light amber contents. "Because," he said slowly after a while, "contrary to that popular perception I mentioned, like you, we're sometimes a little frightened by our good fortune and perhaps humbled by it, too.''

He stopped fingering the glass and looked up. ''That's why we do our best to share the wealth,'' he said. ''To welcome those seeking entry.''

Susanna's eyes glowed. ''I, better than anyone, can attest to that.''

''And to support those who want and need our help.''

''Oh, yes...''

''We talked of Thanksgiving, remember?''

''Hmm. *Erntedankfest*.''

''Yes. Except it's not just a *Fest* about *Ernte*, a good harvest, here with us,'' Jeffrey said. ''It's the day we remember our beginnings and count *all* of our blessings....''

Thanksgiving. Turkey Day.

Susanna's nose couldn't stop twitching; a cornucopia of good smells had assaulted it since the previous day.

Pumpkin pie, fragrant with cinnamon, cloves and other—to Susanna's unspoiled nostrils—exotic spices. Who could have thought that that fat orange thing full of slimy strings and slippery seeds would yield such a tempting dessert? And that those seeds, once lightly toasted with a sprinkling of salt, would be such fun to munch?

Elaine had made walnut pie, too, redolent with the fragrance of carameled sugar.... Sweet potatoes, a vegetable Susanna had never heard of, and those things called marshmallows that Elaine was arranging on top.

"You're going to make yourself sick," Jeffrey warned indulgently. Susanna, who was busily chopping vegetables for coleslaw, popped yet another of the plump, fluffy white confections into her mouth. Her sweet tooth never ceased to amaze him. "Me, I'm usually okay until *after* the dinner."

"These days, maybe," Elaine chimed in with a laugh. "But I can remember plenty of times when you were younger—"

"Mother!" Jeff playfully slapped her on the hand. "That'll do. Susanna's heard all the tales she can stomach for a while."

"Says you!" Elaine batted his hand away from the lid of the pot he was about to peer into. "Don't you have a football game to watch or something?"

"It's not on yet."

"Go watch the parade, then."

"I don't want to." Jeff wanted to be near Susanna. He glanced at her again; she looked adorably domestic with one of his mother's aprons tied over a very becoming red wool dress. "How about I check the turkey for you?"

"How about you get out of my kitchen?" countered Elaine. She turned, obviously registered where his attention lay, raised a brow and added, "And take Susanna with you. She's been helping me all morning and I wouldn't want her to think Thanksgiving is all work and no play. Take a hike, you two."

"But, Mrs. Kent," Susanna protested. "I'm not done with this cabbage and, anyway, it's raining out there...."

"Never mind, Susanna." Jeff took the chopping knife from her hand and, his face only inches from hers, reached around to untie and tug off the apron. "Mother didn't mean for us to hike outside. She just wants us to get lost. Out of her way."

Clasping her shoulders, he turned her toward the door and gave her a little shove. "So scoot. And I'm right behind you."

As if Susanna needed to be told. Even without his hands on her, she could feel Jeff down every inch of her back.

Her eyes sought Elaine's. "Are you sure you don't need me?"

"Oh, yes, dear. Quite sure." Elaine looked thoughtful, but Susanna caught a glimpse of a smile lurking around the corners of her mouth. "But I'm beginning to think Jeffrey does."

Jeffrey's sister, Joanne, and her husband Carl Seeger arrived with their two children about an hour later. Jeff and Susanna were sitting on the floor in front of the family room TV. A football rule book lay open on Susanna's lap. Ronald Kent sat in his customary recliner, looking indulgent. A cheery wood fire crackled and popped in the fireplace, its flames reflected in the brightness of Susanna's gaze, glued to the action on the television screen.

"Touchdown!" she yelled, bouncing up and down along with the fans in the stands, excitement making her temporarily oblivious to the Seegers' arrival.

"No, it wasn't," Jeff contradicted, adding with a scowl, "though I sure think it should've been. Was that a foul, Dad? Number 23?"

"I really couldn't say, son."

"But why isn't it a touchdown?" Susanna demanded heatedly. "You said if the fellow runs all the way to the end with the ball—"

Jeff cut her off. "Yes, but didn't you see? The guy was tackled just before—"

"No, no, you're wrong." She waved the rule book in his face. "He was already over the line when he fell and dropped the ball."

"Was not!"

"The ref agrees with Susanna," said Ron mildly from his seat in the corner. He used the remote to mute the sound of the game, then winked at the rest of his family and added more loudly, "Sure glad to see you, Joanne and Carl."

Jeff and Susanna abruptly ceased arguing, turning swiftly as a little girl's voice piped, "But aren't you glad to see me'n Kimmy, too, Gampa?"

The adults began to laugh, and Ron wordlessly held open his arms for the red-headed, curly-haired dynamo who had just spoken.

"Hey, what about me?" Jeff protested, vaulting lithely onto his feet and tugging up Susanna, too. "Don't I get a hug?"

"Uncle Jeff's usually numero uno in Elly's book," Joanne Seeger explained to Susanna. Holding out her hand, she added, "Hi. I'm his much nicer sister, Joanne."

"I've looked forward to meeting you." Susanna liked the other woman immediately and envied her the baby straddling Joanne's hip. "And who's this little treasure?" she cooed, smiling.

"This is Kim." Susanna saw Joanne glow with maternal pride and drop a peck on top of the child's downy head. "She's almost six months old."

"What a precious." Susanna held out her hands. "May I?"

"Gladly." The baby changed hands and Joanne huffed a sigh. "Little turkey's getting heavy."

"Ahh." Carefully holding the baby, who was eyeing her solemnly but without alarm, Susanna turned to smile at Jeffrey and caught him staring at her with the oddest expression. She felt her own smile freeze at the sight of the almost brooding expression he wore.

Then Elly launched herself at him and Jeff, catching her, laughed—and the moment might never have been.

In all it had been a wonderful day, Susanna reflected, readying for bed several hours later. Never had she eaten such a sumptuous meal or experienced a day filled with such togetherness. What a wonderful family they were, these Kents, and how graciously each one of them had made her feel a part of it. She wished she really could be. Wished Joanne were her sister, Elaine her mother....

No. Maria was the only mother Susanna truly ever wanted to have. And as for Jeffrey...

Susanna dreamily tugged the brush through her hair. No. My brother is not what I long for Jeffrey to be. My friend, yes. My lover, oh, yes. Yes. Perhaps even my husband, and—

She thought of little Kim. How good it had felt to hold her! Closing her eyes, she imagined the baby as her own and Jeffrey as the father. She saw herself pregnant with his child, imagined him coming to stand behind her and enfold her in a belly-to-back embrace. She felt his hands on the roundness of her tummy, sensed him smile as the baby moved at his touch....

Träumerin!

Suddenly impatient with herself and her silly daydreams, Susanna tossed aside the brush and resolutely set about folding down the bedspread. You came to America to find your father, she reminded herself sternly, not a husband. Remember that, you silly goose.

Yes, but when will my father call? Will he ever?

Watching through the window of his garage apartment, Jeffrey watched the wind whip the blue-black curls around Susanna's head into a riot. She was leaning into the wind, buttoning her coat as she walked away from the house. Something in the set of her shoulders and in the purposeful briskness of her stride left him with no doubt that she was on some mission of importance she had set for herself.

Jeff briefly debated going out after her, but decided to leave well enough alone. He was no youngster, no longer intent on carving notches on his bedpost. At thirty-five, he had learned some time ago that not every woman he found attractive and desired needed to be his and was therefore fair game.

But even without that bit of mature insight, Susanna Jaeger could never have been only "fair game." Though she was able without conscious effort to make him hum as no other woman ever had, she had enough on her plate to deal with right now. Besides that, she was a woman who was looking for a home and roots.

Only yesterday she had told him so again, at length and in great detail.

Jeff had invited Susanna along while he ran some errands for his mother, because he knew what a kick she got out of such mundane pursuits as squeezing fruit—"They'd cane your fingers for that in Germany!"—choosing detergent and studying the labels of cereal boxes.

"Junk," she'd declare, taking boxes out of their cart just as fast as Jeff could toss in all his favorite brands. "Loaded with tropical oils and sodium, lacking in fiber—"

"And this from a woman who dumps four spoons of sugar into one cup of coffee!"

"Too much fat." Out went the steak he had chosen.

"Marbled just right." Back in it went.

"Wonderful broccoli."

"Don't you dare bring that home...."

Shopping had never been so much fun. Laughing, tussling over ice cream versus frozen yogurt, Jeff had teased, "You've got all the makings of the classic *hausfrau,* Miss Jaeger."

"Why thank you, Mr. Kent." She'd beamed, taking what he'd intended as a little dig for a compliment. "One day I hope to be one."

He'd rolled his eyes. "What a waste."

"How can you say that?" she exclaimed. "It's a wonderful thing for a woman to take care of her man and his home. It's what I want more than anything...."

"And here I thought finding your father was."

"It is. That's been my dream." She'd grown still, a faraway look in her eyes. "But at Thanksgiving, holding little Kim in my arms, feeling her soft body and smelling her sweet hair, I was reminded of another dream I used to have as I grew up solitary and alone. My stepfather, my only security, was rarely at home. He traveled all the time on behalf of the party. And I would dream then of one day having not just one child but several. Of the man who'd be their father. A good man, strong, steadfast and loving...."

She'd raised her eyes to his, searching them and added, "A man who, unlike my father and stepfather, will be there. For the children as well as for me...."

Well. Jeff turned from the window and restlessly paced the room. He was certainly not that man. Not now. Not ever. He had tried to be once and had ended up hurting not only himself but the woman he'd married, as well. Jill was married again now, to a banker with regular hours and habits, not a crazed journalist like himself, eager to run from wife and bed at every screech of a siren.

No. Jeff sighed, for the first time not as sure of the rightness of his convictions as he once had been, but still adamant with himself, nonetheless. One call from Roy Everson and he'd be out the door like a horse out of the starting gate, adrenaline pumping, running like the wind to chase the next story.

That was why, however much as the thought of some fast and furious loving with Susanna might appeal and tantalize—and it did—he was going to observe the hands-off policy he had decided to impose upon himself. Which meant keeping away from Susanna as much as possible for the rest of her short stay in his parents' home.

Chapter Five

At first, her pace brisk, Susanna merely walked to work some of the pent-up frustrations out of her system. But pretty soon the quiet neighborhood streets seemed too quiet, so she hopped onto a bus that was headed downtown, hoping that the noise and bustle there would provide some distraction. There she walked again, aimlessly and without really taking in her surroundings, up Fourth Avenue, down Yesler, through Pioneer Square.

When she stopped and looked around, she found herself in front of the police station. As she stood and stared at its facade of old and dirty red bricks, she sensed that this was where she had meant to come all along. She needed to talk to someone, and who better than Detective Golding? She needed to assure herself that the authorities really were doing everything they could to reach her father. She had been at the Kents' for too long. Jeffrey Kent was growing too dear, too important. It was time to move on.

"Detective Golding," she said to the desk sergeant. "Is he in?"

The officer checked a roster, nodded, and began to hoist himself out of his chair. "Here, I'll—"

"No, I'm fine," Susanna interrupted. "Thank you. I know the way."

She found Barney on the phone, feet propped on the straight-backed chair at the side of his desk and the customary, half-smoked cigar sticking out of the side of his mouth. Spotting Susanna, he motioned for her to come in, removing his feet and waving her toward the chair. Keeping his pale blue, slightly bloodshot and watery eyes on hers as she sat down, he ended his conversation, replaced the phone and said, "So what's up?"

By now Susanna had gotten somewhat used to American casualness in general and Barney Golding's brusque manner in particular. She had also learned that the question he'd just asked by way of a greeting had nothing to do with things in the air, on the ceiling or otherwise aloft. It was simply another way of asking, "What can I do for you?"

Sitting there in front of him, she suddenly had no reply. After all, if he'd had any news for her, he would have let her know, wouldn't he?

With an embarrassed little smile, she shrugged. "I was restless. The waiting..." She looked down; her fingers were twisting the belt of her raincoat into a corkscrew. Then she glanced up. "It's been—"

"Ten days, I know."

Susanna drew courage from his gruffly gentle tone and fierce frown which, on any other face, might have been taken for displeasure. On Barney Golding's freckled features, however, they were clearly expressions of reluctant sympathy.

"By any chance could you, would you be able to... to check with someone?" she inquired, leaning toward him in an attitude of supplication. "Perhaps they, the others, have heard something and just haven't thought to let us know. I mean, this is a relatively minor matter to such an important government agency and surely—"

Barney's silent shake of the head cut short the rest of Susanna's speech. Unnerved by a sudden rush of pressure behind her eyelids, she lowered her head and blinked rapidly. She couldn't, she wouldn't cry. Not here, not now. Not after all these years without tears.

"Jeff know you're here?"

Susanna didn't look up at Barney's question. She shook her head as she worked to swallow the lump of pain in her throat.

"Why don't I give him a call?" Barney went on. "Have him pick you up."

"No." Not Jeffrey again. He was already too much involved in her life. She had come to depend on him more than she should and was already too much in his and his family's debt. And though she knew kindness and generosity would prompt him to come, by now he doubtlessly felt he'd done more than enough already. And he had.

She stood. "It's all right, I..." She straightened the chair, took a step backward and lifted her eyes to Barney's. The empathy she saw there tightened her throat anew. "Thank you," she said softly. Turning, she left the cubicle before Barney could make a reply.

Outside, Susanna stood for a moment, not sure where to go from there. She couldn't go back to the Kents', not yet, not feeling the way she did. She was full of despair, and choking on a sense of hopelessness the like of which she had not felt even when things had been at their bleakest, back in Linzberg, after her mother's death.

A gust of chilling wind off the water made her shiver. She wrapped her thin raincoat more securely around herself and, spotting the sign of a coffee shop two doors down, walked the few paces and went in.

"Just coffee, please," Susanna told the waitress, who was at her side before she could even scrape back the chair at the Formica-topped corner table she chose. With the lunch rush over, the place was empty. A potpourri of smells from the daily deep-fried specials still lingered in the air. Bruce Springsteen bewailed his hometown.

"There you go, hon." The waitress, a woman of indeterminate age with an improbable hair color, loudly cracked her chewing gum and set down a mug. "Cream 'n sugar's on the table."

Susanna thanked her absentmindedly. Stirring sugar into the blackish-brown liquid, she turned her head to stare unseeingly at the street, deep in thought. It was time, she told herself. Time for her to face facts.

It was time to take stock, realistically, of her situation and come to grips with the possibility of failure. It was time to mentally and emotionally prepare herself for taking leave of this place, this country, which had come to mean so much to her in the two short weeks she had been there.

America. Her father's country of birth and allegiance. It was everything she had always dreamed it would be—and so much more. It was boisterous, busy, big. It was beautiful. She didn't want to leave. Perhaps she would have been better off if she'd never come.

But then she would never have known Jeffrey Kent.

The thought was unexpected, and the one that followed it caused Susanna a sense of loss very much like the one she had felt at her mother's death. *When you leave, you'll never see him again.*

The strength of her feelings shocked, but no longer surprised her. She had never been one to form friendships easily, being by nature reserved and having been taught caution by the conditions within which she'd grown up.

How strange, then, that she should feel as if in this man, this *American*, she had somehow found a soul mate. A friend. Someone she could trust and even— Susanna frowned before hesitantly completing the thought—perhaps even care for....

Lost in her bittersweet reverie, it took Susanna a moment to register that someone had stopped outside the cafe window and was watching her. A man. A tall man whose russet hair was being mussed by the wind and whose green eyes behind steel-framed glasses were narrowed, their expression thoughtful.

Jeffrey.

Susanna felt a rush of gladness more warming than the coffee she'd been cautiously sipping, but no surprise at seeing him there.

Perhaps she'd hoped he would come. Perhaps that was why she'd come into this café and sat by the window.

She offered him a tentative smile. He didn't return it. Instead he turned, walked through the front door and up to her table.

"Mind if I sit?" he asked, scraping back the chair opposite and seating himself before she could reply. "Hot tea," he said to the approaching waitress. Briskly rubbing his hands, he added to Susanna, "Chilly out there, isn't it?"

Susanna made no reply to this bit of small talk, so they sat and looked at each other in silence for several almost audible heartbeats. The memories they had forged during their brief association—memories of kisses and touches and laughter shared—infused the lengthening eye contact with a magnetic quality, making it impossible for either of them to look away.

Jeff's tea arrived. Released from their charged, mutual contemplation, her hand not quite steady, Susanna picked up her own mug of coffee and sipped with pretended nonchalance. She was thinking with a horrified kind of wonder how very easy it would be to toss aside common sense with a man as extraordinary as Jeffrey Kent! And how very, very much she wanted at that moment to ask him to hold and kiss her again. For comfort, yes, but for other reasons, too.

"D-did Detective Golding telephone you?" she asked nervously when Jeff seemed disinclined to do more than sit there, bobbing his tea bag up and down. What was he thinking?

His thoughts would have shocked her, had she known them, for the lingering contact between Susanna's large, doelike eyes and his own had steered Jeffrey's thoughts inexorably toward the bedroom. Susanna's dark beauty was immensely attractive to him. He ached to bury his hands in the wealth of her ebony hair, spent his nights longing to bare the tawny skin of her body and hungering to feel it hot against his own. The sense of loss he was feeling at the realization that none of that could ever be possible deeply troubled and dismayed him.

Vaguely aware that Susanna had spoken, he raised his head, frowning. "I'm sorry, what . . . ?"

To Susanna, Jeff suddenly seemed angry. Had her eyes betrayed her? she worried. Had they let him see the tender feelings for him she was struggling against, and were they as troubling and unwelcome to him as they were to her? It would seem so.

Unaccountably wounded, she nevertheless straightened in her seat with all the dignity she could muster. "It wasn't at all necessary for Detective Golding to call, or for you to come downtown after me," she said. "I would much prefer not to trouble you any more than I already have these past weeks. In fact—"

"Your father called right after you left," Jeff interrupted. He had gone over to the house for a sandwich when the phone had rung. He had taken the call . . . and ever since that brief exchange with the former Harry Miller, he had been struggling to come to grips with the realization that until that moment he had secretly nourished the hope that Susanna's father wouldn't be found. "He said he'd phone again at four o'clock."

"What?!"

Her father had called. He had called!

"F-four o'clock?" Susanna leaped to her feet. "Jeffrey! What time is it? We've got to go. Do you have your car? What if no one's there when he telephones? Hurry...."

Practically incoherent with shock and excitement, she would have rushed right out the door, but Jeff caught her by the arm.

"Whoa," he said past a funny, almost painful lump of tenderness in his throat. Susanna's face was flushed, her eyes bright; she looked like a kid at Christmas. And was obviously not a bit sorry to be shortly leaving him.

"It's only two. There's ample time...."

"But there's so much to do...."

"Like what?" Rising, Jeff dropped a couple of bills onto the table and, still holding Susanna's arm, steered her toward the exit.

"My clothes... I've got to change.... Perhaps a dress. That red one I wore on Thanksgiving... Oh, Jeffrey."

Already halfway out the door, she stopped and faced him, gripping the front of his leather flyer's jacket with both hands. "Please. Tell me how..." She couldn't speak for a moment; fear threatened to close her throat. "H-how did he seem to you, Jeffrey? H-how did he sound, what did he say?"

Jeff heard the tremor in her voice and could guess at the awful uncertainty she had to be feeling. To know that the fulfillment of her dream was imminent, yet suddenly wonder if happiness would necessarily follow. Some dreams ended in heartache....

But not this one, damn it.

"He sounded fine," he told Susanna, catching her ice-cold hands in his and gently prying them from his jacket. He pressed them reassuringly and added, "Eager to talk to you and disappointed when he heard you weren't there."

"Really?" Some of Susanna's tension left. Hope rekindled, she smiled at Jeff and caught an expression very much like regret on his face. She felt her smile fade. With a rush of fervent feeling, she returned the pressure of his hands. "You have been so very kind," she told him. "Never will I forget your kindness."

Or you.

She didn't say those last words, but they were there in her heart and almost on her tongue.

In just a day or two she would be leaving this man. She would be on her way to her father, and to whatever fate had in store for her after that. With the help of her father she would be granted permission to stay in this country. She would live with or near him, at least for a while. At least until they'd had a chance to get to know one another, to really become father and daughter.

Family. If it wasn't quite the one she had come to dream of here with Jeffrey, at least she would no longer be alone.

She would find a job—surely nurses were as much in demand in this country as they had been in hers? She would get more schooling, if that was required or simply start at the bottom. She wouldn't mind that. She was a good nurse; she loved her job and had always genuinely cared about the well-being of her patients. It would show; she would prosper and advance.

She would make a good life for herself. Unclasping her hands from Jeffrey's and dredging up another smile, Susanna stepped back. She would be happy.

After all but wearing a rut in the den's carpeting, Susanna turned into a statue when the telephone finally rang. Completely unable to move, she could only stand there and stare at the apparatus as if at some ghastly demon. One, two... She inwardly counted each shrill ring. Three, four, five... She could still make no move to answer it. On eight it stopped in midring.

He had given up. Good God! She had just stood there and she'd lost her chance! One hand flew to her mouth. She spun to stare wildly at the door that had just opened.

"Your father's on the line, my dear," Elaine Kent said gently, clearly taking in Susanna's distraught state at a glance. "Here." She pressed her onto a chair and handed her the phone. "Go ahead. Talk to him."

Hesitant, her movements jerky, Susanna shakily lifted the receiver and brought it to her ear. "H-hello?" she said in little more than a hoarse whisper. There was a soft click on the line; Elaine must have hung up in the other room. Her heart was hammering so loudly, it was a wonder she'd even heard it. Certainly she heard nothing else, except... a shuddering sort of exhalation from the other end of the line.

"Hello?" she ventured again, firming her voice. Could it be her father was every bit as nervous and afraid as she was? She swallowed, trying to ease the dryness in her mouth, conjuring up in her mind his likeness from the locket. It was as dear and familiar to her as the one of her mother next to it. "This, uh," she said. "This is Susanna...."

"Susanna." Her name was little more than yet another raggedly released breath, yet it was spoken in a tone full of wonder and disbelief.

Susanna gripped the receiver more tightly, closing her eyes against a sudden rush of tears. There was no time for tears now. She had to be able to speak, to reach out....

"Father," she said, choking up in spite of her best intentions.

"My daughter." Her father, too, seemed overcome by powerful emotions. His voice was rough; it broke a little as he spoke. "How I've longed for this day. Are you all right?"

"I'm wonderful, now that I hear your voice."

"I know the feeling." He wheezed a chuckle, then grew concerned again. "But where are you, Susanna? Who are these people you're staying with?"

Susanna sketched the Kents for him in broad strokes, taking care, however, not to betray the depth of her feelings for their son. "They've been most gracious," she concluded. "I really don't know how I could have managed without them."

"Thank God for people like them," Harry Miller said. "I owe them a world of gratitude."

"And I, too."

There was a pause, then Miller said, "When can I see you?"

"Anytime you say." Tears coursed unheeded down Susanna's cheeks. She was clutching the phone with both hands, her body curled around it as if in an embrace. "As soon as you want."

"How soon can you get here, child? I... I'm in Southern California, I can't give you anything more specific than that over the phone. They, the people you've been dealing with on this, will give you all the particulars. Please understand...."

"I do."

"They feel it's still a necessity."

"I understand. Truly."

"You're a very beautiful woman," her father said softly—Susanna had sent a photo of herself along with the locket. "Your mother's features and my own mother's hair and eyes. I'd have known you anywhere."

"And I you," Susanna said feelingly.

At that he chuckled, if indeed the few short rasps he made could be called a chuckle. "I doubt it, child. I doubt it."

His name had been changed to Francis Christian King.

"It became expedient," Agent Arthur Kirkland of the FBI explained to Susanna. "A matter of securing your father's well-being. Here—" He jotted something on a piece of paper and handed it to her. "Here's his address and phone number."

Susanna glanced at it. 1910 San Miguel Drive, West Hollywood, California. "Thank you." She folded it carefully and put it away.

Turning to go, she saw Kirkland tip back his chair, hands folded across a lean middle. "Miss Jaeger," he said.

Doorknob in hand, Susanna looked back. "Yes?"

"The cold war may be over, but there's still a couple of people around who'd give anything to get their hands on your old man. There've been indications that lead us to believe it is known that you're Harry Miller's daughter. Any ideas how that's possible?"

"N-no. Unless—"

"What?" Kirkland said sharply. "Unless what?"

"Unless it's somehow through my stepfather, Thomas Jaeger. When he was still alive, he once made inquiries."

"I see." Clearly not pleased, Kirkland let the chair land on all fours. "Damn fool, I told him not to do this."

"You knew Thomas Jaeger?" Susanna asked incredulously.

"No, I don't. Didn't. I'm talking about Harry Miller." Kirkland scowled at her. "I told him not to see you, but he wouldn't listen, and there's only so much I can do. A word of advice, young lady—do not trust anyone, keep your eyes open and your mouth shut. The less you talk about this whole thing, the better for everyone concerned."

Shaken, Susanna could only nod. Her legs not quite steady, she stepped into the wide, vaulted corridor of the government building and, her footsteps echoing hollowly, walked slowly toward the exit.

Halfway down the dozen or so wide steps leading to the sidewalk stood Barney Golding. Hands buried in the pockets of a soiled, shapeless overcoat, cigar stub in mouth, he squinted at her.

"So you got it," he said, when Susanna was abreast of him.

She was surprised to see him and said so.

He shrugged, falling into step as she continued down the steps. "Kent called me, and right after that, Kirkland was on the horn to say contact had been made. Strictly courtesy, y'understand, since this really isn't a police matter."

"I see." They were on the sidewalk. Unsure of what the detective wanted from her, but sensing that he wasn't there simply to chat, Susanna stopped.

Golding did, too, saying, "Do you? I wonder."

He took the stub from his mouth, studied it for a moment, then tossed it into a nearby trash bin. "Filthy things," he said, fishing in a breast pocket and coming out with a fresh one. "If I had any sense I'd give 'em up. But then..." He bit off the tip, spat it out, then puffed as he held a match to it. "If I had any sense I'd be a schoolteacher instead of a cop, so what the hell."

He smoked for a moment, staring into space, then looked back at Susanna. "So what're your plans, Miss Jaeger? Hop on the next plane out of town for the grand reunion, I s'pose, eh?"

"Actually," Susanna said, still puzzled, "the next *bus* was more like what I had in mind. In fact, I'm on my way to the station to inquire about timetables and such."

"Plane, bus, whatever." Barney shrugged off the technicality. "The point is you'll be hotfooting it over to wherever dear old Dad is holed up, and you oughta know that this ain't just your everyday jaunt to Grandma's house."

Accustomed by now to the detective's unorthodox way of speaking, Susanna didn't even try to interpret his words literally, but even so she was lost. "Grandma's house?'' she queried, bewildered. "I don't understand."

"That's exactly what I'm talking about. You don't understand." Golding yanked the cigar from his mouth and jabbed the air with it, then lowered his voice and spoke emphatically. "Your father was more than just a spy, Miss Jaeger. He was a double agent with a price on his head."

At Susanna's shocked gasp, Barney gripped her elbow and propelled her toward an older model gray sedan. "My car," he said, opening the door on the passenger side and all but shoving her in. "I'll drive you to the damn bus depot, but you listen to me...."

As soon as they were away from the curb and merging with traffic, Barney continued.

"The Feds, or whoever, yanked him outa East Germany and brought him home to stay as soon as the other side got wind of the fact that Miller had not only been feeding them bogus information, but that he'd been instrumental in the capture of one of their top spies. A real ace, man by the name of Igor Otrovsky."

Barney swerved to avoid another car, roundly cursed the driver, and went right on talking; Susanna sat motionless.

"Now, this Otrovsky got out of the slammer thanks to an exchange of some kind in which your father was instrumental. Word is, nowadays he hangs out in the Middle East somewhere, and his name's been linked to some acts of international terrorism. Two former U.S. agents have been killed in two separate car bombings, both of 'em had dealings with Otrovsky at one time or another, and both of 'em worked with your father.''

He turned a corner and squealed to a halt in front of the bus depot. He cut the engine and turned to Susanna. ''Didn't you or your mother ever wonder why Harry never made contact except for those lousy three letters?''

''Y-yes.'' Maria had often told Susanna she feared for Harry's safety and well-being and about the tears she had shed. Until Thomas Jaeger had come into her life. Thomas, a man of power in the communist party, had discreetly—and reluctantly—made inquiries on Maria and Susanna's behalf. He hadn't been able to glean much, however. The Americans had taken too much care to keep secret Miller's whereabouts and condition, but he *had* learned that Harry was alive.

''We always believed, though,'' Susanna told Barney, ''that he must have had a good reason....''

''The best,'' Barney said dryly. ''Staying alive. They got to him once, you know. He got shot.''

Gott im Himmel! Susanna stared at Barney, aghast. ''Sh-shot? By whom?''

Barney shrugged. ''They figure Otrovsky or one of his henchmen did it. It was a close call, and afterward the Feds made Harry disappear.''

Leaning toward her, Barney put his finger beneath Susanna's chin and made her look at him. There was caring in his bloodshot eyes and concern. ''You got guts, Miss Jaeger, and I admire that. You've made some friends here, and I'd like to think I'm one of them, which is why I'm telling you—this is the big time. What you're involved in here is serious stuff. Make a wrong move and you could get hurt. I wouldn't like that, and neither would Jeffrey Kent. Get the picture?''

Boy, did she. Susanna clenched her teeth to keep them from chattering. By going to her father, she was placing him in the gravest possible danger. By agreeing to see her, he was allowing himself to become vulnerable to attack, to possible assassination. And yet he wanted her to come to him.

Her father loved her. The knowledge warmed and comforted Susanna, but at the same time, considering the risks, distressed her, too. Knowing the possible consequences now, how dare she selfishly go to him, regardless?

How dare she place the fulfillment of a dream, her own pursuit of happiness, ahead of her father's life?

Chapter Six

Jeff didn't know what to do. He paced. Damn Barney Golding, anyway. Swearing, he pounded the wall beside the window with his fist. Where did the guy get off, making him feel responsible for the well-being of a woman he hadn't even known existed a month ago!

Hadn't he done enough for Susanna Jaeger, for crying out loud? Hadn't he rescued her from that dump of a hotel and brought her home to his family? Hadn't he seen to her comfort and entertainment, shown her the town, sacrificed a portion of his hard-earned vacation? And hadn't he just made peace with the idea that letting her go was the only acceptable course of action?

He didn't need this. *Do us both a favor, Kent, and go with her to L.A.*

Damn. Jeff pounded the wall again, his thoughts churning. If he did what Barney asked, it would mean another week or ten days of being near the one woman *to* whom he was more strongly attracted than he'd ever been before, and *with* whom he could never pursue that attraction. Who the hell needed that kind of aggravation?

Sighing, he let his forehead drop onto his fist.

She was in danger, Barney had said. A gut feeling, Barney had said. Jeff cursed again, at length. *Damn* Barney Golding's gut feelings. And damn the fact that they'd seldom been wrong.

Jeff went to find Susanna.

"Upstairs, dear," his mother told him when he asked. "And you might as well know dinner'll be ready in fifteen minutes."

Dinner was the last thing on Jeff's mind as he stood in the open door to Joanne's room and looked at Susanna.

She was packing. Thanks to her latest foray into the mall with his mother, she now owned quite a few more clothes than she had on her arrival. Jeff happened to know that Elaine had insisted on paying for most of those purchases. Now, the almost reverent care with which Susanna was folding them into her cheap little suitcase touched his heart; it was clear that beautiful things of any kind had been all too scarce in her life.

Scanning her willowy length, he couldn't help but notice that she no longer resembled the careworn refugee he had met on the airplane. Dressed in warm leggings and an oversize multicolored sweater, her luxurious hair caught in a ponytail from which the usual willful curls stuck out in all directions, she looked quite American, very beautiful, wholesome and at the same time provocatively seductive.

The combination took his breath away, making his voice husky as he softly spoke her name.

Susanna had not heard Jeffrey approach, but her thoughts—as they all too often were—had been on him.

She couldn't have said how and when it had happened, but at some point during the past weeks Jeffrey Kent had become an important part of her life. His pointed withdrawal from her over the past day or two had therefore been all the more bewildering, and painful.

Lost in her musings, the sound of Jeff's voice from right next to her caused Susanna to start. She snapped to attention—"Jeffrey!"—thinking her musings might have conjured him up.

The way Susanna had breathed his name—awed, almost reverently—took Jeff aback. He swept his eyes over her once more, before allowing them to linger on her softly parted lips. The old Susanna had been lovely, he thought, but this new one was glorious.

And he wanted her.

Abruptly looking away, feeling shaky, he sucked in a deep lungful of air. It was agony, this wanting, when he knew without a doubt that Susanna could never be his. She came from a different world, one that had left her with needs, emotional needs, he'd never be able to meet. She dreamed dreams he had long since decided not to pursue.

She longed for stability, a home and roots. He had become a Gypsy and liked it that way. She longed for love, the forever-after variety, and she would expect—and deserve—that kind of commitment from a man.

He, on the other hand, was no longer into commitments outside of his job. That job being what it was, he had become a "Hi-Goodbye-It's-Been-Fun" kind of guy and knew himself well enough to know that this wasn't likely to change. That knowledge brought no comfort; on the contrary, it caused a sense of loss that was as surprising as it was painful.

Susanna had seen Jeffrey's frown and, not knowing the cause, but attributing it to herself, she quickly went back to her packing. What was it about her, she wondered dismally, that lately always seemed to bring this look of dismay to Jeffrey's eyes whenever he looked at her? Something she'd said? Or done? Had he—during moments of reflection—been repulsed by her eager response to his kisses, his touch? Did he think she was easy, or, God forbid, out to ensnare him in some way?

She had heard that people sometimes married American citizens for the sole purpose of gaining permanent residence in the United States....

She gasped, appalled. *Um Gottes Willen!*

Could Jeffrey possibly be suspecting her of similarly self-serving motives? Did he think she had played up to him in order to secure for herself—what was the expression?—an ace in the hole? In case things didn't work out with her father?

Horrified by the very idea, and devastated by the notion that Jeff might think her so callous, Susanna slanted him a quick, bright smile that severely strained her acting skills. She had always been as transparent as glass where her emotions were concerned, but in this instance pride forbade her to let him see how much his visible reserve wounded her.

"As you can see," she said, clumsily folding the last of her possessions, the threadbare gray suit, into the suitcase with hands that shook, "I'm almost packed and ready to go. My bus departs the depot at eight in the morning."

She straightened, made herself face him, and willed her voice not to quiver. "I want you to know how very much I appreciate all you've done on my behalf, Jeffrey. I can never thank you enough...."

"No thanks are necessary."

Jeff was irked by her straight-backed coolness. Obviously the thought of leaving Seattle and his family, the thought of leaving *him*, was causing Susanna no heartache at all. But then he saw the sheen of moisture in the eyes she hastened to avert and instantly regretted his peevish tone. One long step put him in front of her.

"What's this?" he said, catching her chin and gently urging her face up to his. "Tears? At a time like this?" He clicked his tongue in mock reproof. "Susanna, you'll soon be with your father, remember? In just a few short days. You should be happy...."

"I am." But her voice broke, and she wouldn't look at him; a tear rolled slowly down her cheek.

Jeff caught the tear with his thumb and framed her face with both hands. "But?" he prompted softly.

Susanna bit her lip and vehemently shook her head. She continued to avoid his gaze, but Jeff wouldn't have it. "Tell me," he said, catching her chin once again and forcing it up. "Tell me what's wrong, Susanna. Let me help, if I can."

"No." She pulled out of his grip. "I don't need any more help, and especially not from you."

Taken aback by her vehemence, Jeff dropped his hands.

Susanna looked at him then and caught his affronted expression. Clearly she had hurt Jeffrey's feelings and this pained her, but she was determined to make him understand that she had never expected anything from him beyond simple friendship.

"You've done enough," she insisted. "You've done more than I would ever have dared to ask, in fact. I never expected, never intended—"

At a loss for the right words, she broke off, continuing to beseech him with her eyes. "I never wanted anything at all from you, Jeffrey," she said finally.

The words were like salt on an already tender wound, but the imploring way Susanna uttered them, as well as the message he read in her eyes, made Jeffrey bite back a stinging retort. "What are you saying, Susanna?"

Tears welled up. Susanna swallowed to hold them back. "The things between us . . . the kisses—"

"Yes?" Jeff said encouragingly when she stopped and bit her lip. Now he was intrigued as well as bewildered.

"You've been so distant these past couple of days, so cool. And it occurred to me . . ."

She sent him an agonized look that he countered with one of incomprehension. Suddenly fed up with herself and her cowardly evasions, Susanna took a deep breath and blurted, "No matter what happens between my father and me, I have never had any intention of getting you or anyone else to marry me as a consequence." She lifted her chin proudly. "So you can just stop worrying about that, all right?"

Completely at a loss, Jeff could only frown. Susanna's face was flushed, her expression strained, but the fervor in her voice and the fire in her eyes left him with no doubt that the announcement she'd just made was—to her—an important one. One she fully expected him to understand and be reassured by.

"All right," he said at length, nodding his head and speaking reasonably and quietly, as if addressing an overwrought child. "Just what *are* your intentions then?"

"My intentions are to ask the government for permission to stay in this country, regardless. Since I *am* the daughter of an American citizen, this should be entirely possible. On the off chance that my request would not be granted, I..."

She shrugged and, in a gesture Jeff was beginning to recognize as characteristic, looked down at her hands, before resolutely meeting his gaze once again. "But no," she said. "I refuse to entertain that possibility. Suffice it to say that I never expected *you* to marry me so that I may stay."

"Well, that's a relief," Jeff quipped; understanding had finally dawned and with it, amusement. He'd meant the remark to be flippantly humorous, to indicate he'd never attached that kind of interpretation to the pleasurable moments they'd shared, but one look at Susanna's expression made it clear their communication gap had widened again.

"I'm sorry, Susanna." He raked a hand through his hair and sighed. "It seems to me we've somehow gotten onto a treadmill of misunderstandings here and keep going round and round. Let me make my position clear to you, all right? And maybe then we can move on to more important things. Like dinner.''

He checked off each point on his fingers. "One, I helped you out because I've been damn glad of a helping hand in foreign countries myself from time to time. Two, I kissed you simply because I wanted to, and because, at the time, the moment seemed to call for it. Period. I did not read any ulterior motive into your very gratifying and flattering response. And three, the reason I'm upstairs here offering more help is because, well, because Barney Golding seems to think you need protection and, frankly, I agree.''

"Protection?"

"Yes. As I know he told you, there is still a very formidable enemy of your father's on the loose. The man has a very long memory and an even longer arm. In spite of the easing of tensions between East and West, this man—Otrovsky—for reasons of his own still seems bent on settling a score with your father. And, from what Barney has told me, it wouldn't bother Otrovsky in the least to kill Harry Miller's daughter if she got in the way.''

Jeff took her hands, and gently stroking the backs of them with his thumb, pinned her with a penetrating gaze. "I wouldn't want anything to happen to you, Susanna.''

Entranced by the throaty huskiness in Jeff's voice and mesmerized by the intensity of his expression, Susanna gazed back at him. "You wouldn't?" she breathed.

Jeff shook his head, his eyes still locked on hers.

"Why?"

"Because I care." That lifted Susanna's heart, then Jeff softly added, "As a friend."

She forced a smile, grateful, yet suddenly melancholy, too. She caught herself thinking, *If only* but banished the words as quickly as they had come. "Thank you," she said with bittersweet sincerity. "I value your friendship more than anything."

Susanna's words, spoken with such feeling, along with the sadness Jeff glimpsed in her beautiful eyes, made him long to gather her close and keep her there. But what good would that do?

Gritting his teeth, he hardened his heart and released her hands.

"So here's what we'll do," he told her, forcing a businesslike tone. "I will drive you to Los Angeles, and I'll see you safely to your father's side. We'll take our time, avoid lonely places, and act like we're just another couple on a vacation jaunt to Tinseltown."

Just another couple. As he said it, their eyes met with a swift and stark awareness.

"For appearances' sake we'll have to share a room when we stop for the night," Jeff continued, forcing the words past suddenly constricted vocal cords. "But don't worry, there's no need for us to share the bed."

"I wouldn't be worried."

"You wouldn't?"

"No, Jeffrey. I trust you. Completely."

They stared at each other for the length of several thundering heartbeats. The expression in Susanna's eyes—so wide, and burning so darkly—made Jeff excruciatingly aware that she was picturing in her mind the same scene he was: the two of them in a hotel room with only one bed. Alone. Naked. . . .

Madness!

Jeff wrenched his eyes from hers and turned away. Gruffly he said, "Well, you damn well shouldn't."

"Jeffrey? Susanna? Dinner's ready, you two!"

"Coming, Mother." Jeff moved toward the door.

"She'll be up here any second, you know, looking for us," Jeff said, looking back at her. Susanna was closing the lid of her suitcase with hands that trembled. "Aren't you coming?"

"In a moment," Susanna said, needing some time to get a grip on her emotions. "You go ahead."

She stayed where she was by the side of the bed until she no longer heard Jeff's footsteps. Then she slowly sank onto the edge of the mattress. Her thoughts scattered in all directions like autumn leaves before the wind.

Jeffrey wanted to go with her to California. He wanted them to pretend to be man and wife. How could she stand it? What should she do?

Hands pressed to her galloping heart, Susanna contemplated this latest development and was forced to admit that she wanted nothing so much as to have Jeffrey with her. A few days more. It was a gift. It would be torture. She couldn't do it, shouldn't allow it. And yet...

What Jeffrey had said to her was right. Hadn't Barney Golding already made it clear that the journey to Los Angeles was very likely to be fraught with peril? Peril for her? Yes. She drew a deep breath and tremblingly released it. But she could cope with that. What she wouldn't be able to bear would be knowing that Jeffrey—if she let him come along—would be in danger, too.

Susanna let her shoulders droop, as if burdened by a terrible load. Her chin dropped to her chest. For long moments she contemplated her no-nonsense, bluntly trimmed fingernails and weighed the question again. Was it right, was it fair, to place one person's dream ahead of two people's—her father's and now Jeffrey's—safety and well-being?

After a while, weary with indecision, she got off the bed and reached for the phone. She knew the number by heart now and swiftly tapped it in. The whir that followed was interrupted by a gruff-voiced, "Hello" at the other end.

"It's Susanna," she said quietly.

The other voice warmed instantly, saying, "Ah. My dear girl. Are you all set?"

Nodding, Susanna glanced at the packed suitcase. "Yes, I am, but—"

Suddenly afraid to put into words the question she had called him to ask, afraid of the answer, she faltered. What if he said, *You're right, it's too risky?* What if he said, *Stay away, don't come?* Would she be able to bear it? Would she be able to do what she would then have to? Go back where she'd come from?

Closing her eyes against a wave of anguish, she gripped the phone and told herself, *Yes.*

"But what, Susanna?" her father asked into the lengthening silence, a note of disquiet now audible in his tone. "Second thoughts at the eleventh hour? Are you afraid the old man won't live up to your expectations?"

"No!" Susanna was aghast at his misinterpretation of her hesitation. "Not at all. Never that. It's just—I wonder if it's really a good idea, my coming to you?''

A pause followed, one in which Susanna's heart pounded furiously in her ears, and which ended with her father's heavy sigh.

"You've changed your mind," he said, and sounded so bitterly resigned that sudden tears stung Susanna's eyes.

"Oh no, Father!" she exclaimed. "That's not it at all. I very much want to come. But there are dangers I hadn't been aware of before—''

"Susanna, listen to me," her father interrupted. "There are dangers, certainly. I can't deny that. And if you're afraid to make this trip, I'll understand. I wouldn't want anything to happen to you."

"Oh, but it's not me I'm worried about."

"Well then don't worry about me, either. Susanna," her father said softly, "I've longed for this for thirty years. And it's not possible for me to come to you, or I would. I want us to be a family, Susanna. I need you.... ''

Nothing could have held Susanna back after that. Hanging up the phone after tender words of parting, she vowed that, come what might, she would reach her father's side and, once there, never leave him again.

I need you. Such sweet, sweet words. Words that, like no others, had the power to reach deep inside her and tug at her tender, nurturing heart.

Scores of the patients she had tended in her years as a nurse had told her she possessed a heart of gold. And while Susanna knew her heart to be as humanly tarnished as anyone else's, she also knew that a cry of need had always brought her running, hands outstretched and ready to help. She could not bear to see anyone hurt or wanting.

Her father needed her so, come what might, she would go to him. But she would go alone.

Having made the decision, for one short moment Susanna gave in to a burst of despair. Knowing that after tomorrow she would never see Jeffrey again, she buried her face in her hands, rocking back and forth, struggling with a grief too strong for tears. How? How in the world had her simple dream become so terribly complicated? And why?

Why was it her fate to be always saying goodbye?

Five o'clock.

Susanna shrugged into her thin little raincoat. She slung her purse over one shoulder and bent to pick up her suitcase and shoes. It was time to go. The taxi she had ordered by phone the night before would be waiting for her a few houses down the block from the Kents'. The note of apology and thanks she had penned to Jeffrey and his family, as well as the money for last night's telephone call to Los Angeles, lay in plain view on the neatly made bed.

Stealthily, noiselessly, Susanna crept down the stairs. Taking care not to bump into anything, she tiptoed across the downstairs entry. Holding her breath, she eased open the heavy front door. For once it didn't creak and, grateful for small mercies, she leaned out and set down her suitcase in the porch. For one long, pain-filled moment she lingered on the threshold and looked back into the dimly lit hall.

There stood the grandfather clock, placidly ticking away the seconds and minutes of each day. There was the large, garish urn, chock-full with an assortment of umbrellas. And above it the slightly tarnished mirror, flanked by pegs to hang coats on. How dear and familiar these objects had become, just as this house and these wonderful people had become the closest thing to a home and family she'd known since her mother's death. It hurt to leave them.

Goodbye, Family Kent, Susanna said silently. *Forgive me for sneaking off like a thief in the night.*

She stepped outside, thinking, *Goodbye, Jeffrey. Don't be angry. You'll never know how much I wish—*

But she firmly shut the door on her sorrow and her wishes, as years of practice had taught her to do. And she reminded herself of a resolution she'd made long ago: only look forward, never back.

Moving briskly now, she dropped her shoes and stepped into them, then picked up her suitcase. Head high, shoulders squared, she turned to go.

Chapter Seven

"Leaving so soon?"

Blinded by a rush of tears she hadn't been able to stem in spite of her resolve not to cry, Susanna didn't immediately see the tall man lounging against the burgundy-colored compact in the driveway. But she would have known the resonant, slightly husky voice anywhere. Jeffrey.

Shocked clear out of her socks by this totally unexpected complication, Susanna dropped her suitcase and stood stock-still, gaping as Jeff pointedly consulted his watch.

"I could've sworn we'd agreed to leave at eight," he drawled, the bite in his silky tone perfectly matching the grim expression Susanna was finally able to make out. "Clearly I misunderstood."

He pushed away from the car and came to her.

"Or maybe I didn't. Which only makes it all the more fortunate that I'm intuitive by nature...." Not missing a beat, he picked up the suitcase, quite matter-of-factly took Susanna by the arm and steered her toward the car. "I had this uncanny premonition that your travel plans might turn out somewhat differently from my, uh, *understanding* of them."

Stowing her bag in the trunk, he caught Susanna's furtive glance up the road and added, "If you're looking for the cab, Susanna, don't bother. I gave the guy a twenty for his trouble and sent him on his way."

Until that moment, Susanna had been too stunned by Jeffrey's unexpected presence to physically react to anything he was saying. She'd been too busy trying to deny what her eyes were seeing to pay attention to what her ears were hearing. Jeff couldn't be here, she'd kept telling herself. This couldn't be him, fully dressed in jeans, turtleneck and beat-up leather jacket, stuffing her luggage into his car.

It took the announcement that he had sent away the taxi—an announcement made in a truly infuriatingly calm, almost bored, tone of voice—to yank her out of her bewildered stupor into reality.

Jeffrey Kent actually *was* out here with her! And he had absolutely no intention of letting her travel to California on her own and thus keep him safe! Worse, by telling her that he'd sent away *her* taxi, he was acting like every other dictatorial male she'd had to cope with in her life!

Like a kettle building a head of steam, Susanna's generally dormant temper began to simmer and, gradually, to boil.

It wasn't until Jeff said, "Now why don't you be a good girl and get in the car so we can get going?" however, that the inevitable explosion occurred.

"I will not!" Furious with him, she wrenched free of his light hold and yanked the suitcase out of the still open trunk. "I most certainly will not be a good girl, and I have no intention of getting into this car. You had no right, Jeffrey Kent, do you hear me? No right at all to send away my taxi..."

"Last night we agreed it's best that I drive you."

She ignored him, barely even stopping to draw breath.

"...and you have no right to be lurking out here at this ungodly hour..."

"Lurking?"

"...when you specifically told me you would sleep till seven-thirty so that you'd be rested for the trip!"

To vent her frustration, Susanna slammed the trunk lid down, but it didn't catch and sprang right up again, bobbing gently.

Glaring first at it, then at Jeffrey, she exclaimed accusingly, "It's as if you didn't trust me, for heaven's sake!"

"I didn't," Jeff countered, "and rightly so!"

"Well, I consider that an insult, given everything that's happened between us."

"Ditto, lady. And in spades." Now Jeff's tightly bottled anger finally blew its cork. Gripping Susanna's shoulders, he shook her like a lumpy pillow. The suitcase she'd kept clutched in her left hand clattered to the ground. "Why can't you get it through that contrary head of yours that it's *because* of what's been happening between us that I want to see you safe?"

"Because I can keep myself safe!"

"It's because I care, damn it!"

He released her so suddenly, Susanna stumbled back a step. "Well, it's, it's because I care, too!" she spluttered.

Moving close again, she gripped his arm and, every bit as angry as he, tried to shake him as he had shaken her. "And I want *you* to understand that it's because I couldn't bear to have anything happen to you that I want to do this alone. You have done enough, Jeffrey Kent, do you hear me?"

Apparently he didn't. Clearly his male ego had been bruised by her attempted deception, because he kept ranting on about contrary women and who needed all this aggravation, anyway. Finally, Susanna could think of only one way of shutting him up.

Growling with impatience, she gripped him by the ears, stretched up on tiptoe and . . . kissed him.

Not gently, and not with passion. Not seductively, and maybe not with her heart. Not like the first time, and certainly not like the last. But even so, Jeff was jolted by the kiss, scorched by it, and—oddly—reassured by it. The bands of steel that had been squeezing his heart ever since he'd seen the cab and had his suspicions confirmed, sprang loose now from the force of her kiss.

His arms, which until then had hung rigidly at his sides, now rose and came around her without conscious direction from his mind. He felt Susanna struggle to pull away, but wouldn't have it. Shifting, he widened his stance, dragged her closer, changed the angle of his head and mouth and took control of the kiss.

At first he, too, wasn't gentle. Lips firm, he dug into hers almost painfully as punishment for the hell she'd put him through. Her small wince of protest made him instantly soften the contact, however, and they kissed deeply then, and softly, until, with a groan, Jeff tore his mouth from hers and sucked in a shuddering breath.

"Susanna," he muttered hoarsely, scattering kisses along her jaw, then burying his face in the fragrant warmth of her neck. "Lord, girl, I've been going crazy."

Tears pricked Susanna's closed eyelids. Her heart, beating every bit as rapidly as Jeff's, swelled painfully with an emotion she dared not identify, one that brought her no joy because—God help her—it was making her selfish. It was urging her to forget the consequences and hold on to Jeffrey, to accept his generosity once again.

How could she go without him? she thought, holding him tight. How could she leave this man who stirred her as no other ever had? How could she get through the rest of her life without having experienced the fullness of their desire at least once?

Jeffrey wanted to come with her. He'd been angry when he'd caught her trying to leave on her own. Would it be so wrong, then, to give in to what they both so badly wanted?

Yes, she answered herself dismally. Yes, it would be wrong. Yet, wrong or not, the die had been cast. Selfishly, she would catch it in her palm and be grateful.

"I'm sorry," she whispered brokenly, holding Jeff tight and, when he kissed her again, openly responding with everything she was feeling, right there for him to see.

"So what is this? Goodbye or hello?" someone asked gruffly beside them.

"Damn it, Golding!" Jeffrey wrenched his lips from Susanna's sweet ones and glared into the rumpled cop's grinning countenance. "What the hell are *you* doing here?"

"I'm taking me a little vacation," Barney said, calmly picking Susanna's dropped suitcase off the driveway and heading for the rusting and battered gray sedan that was his transportation of choice. "And I'm gonna take you two with me. Hollywood or bust."

"What?" Jeff and Susanna chorused. Jeff strode after his friend, exclaiming, "Not in this bucket you're not!"

"If you don't mind." Barney shoved Jeff's hand off the trunk lid none too gently, opened it and tossed in the suitcase. "This bucket, as you so snidely call it, is equipped with the very finest supercharged V-8 engine. And it, my ungrateful friend, can outrun anything on the road."

"If it doesn't fall apart first."

Although he'd been surprised by Barney Golding's unexpected entrance, Jeff was glad to have his friend along on this trip, in spite of his grousing about the car and the fact that he'd really have liked to have Susanna to himself for a few days. Safety in numbers aside, Barney was one helluva cop who knew his business.

Susanna, too, found little to argue about in these new developments. On the contrary, she was both touched by the gruff policeman's concern for her and grateful to him. Now she could continue to enjoy Jeffrey's company without having to worry so much about his safety.

"Thank you," she said warmly. Barney impatiently waved aside her gratitude. "Hell, I needed the break." He chucked the bag Jeff was handing him into the trunk after Susanna's. "You got any idea how long it's been since I took some time off? Get in the car, you two, and let's get goin', all right? Move it...."

By the time the fingers of dawn began to raise the long winter night's curtain of darkness, Susanna, Jeff and Barney were well on their way, heading south past Olympia, Washington State's capital city. The domed capitol building, majestic, and rendered somewhat mysterious by the amber illumination of numerous spot- and footlights, had elicited an awed response from Susanna. Apart from that, however, they'd been driving in comfortable silence.

Barney had taken the wheel, banishing Jeff and Susanna to the back seat. "Get some shut-eye," he'd barked. "It's too damn early for me to socialize."

They hadn't argued, and now, close but not touching, they were content just to sit and follow their own thoughts.

Jeffrey's musings meandered like lost sheep, only to return again and again, with a helpless sort of bewildered dismay, to the unexpected feelings of possessiveness that had added themselves to the mixture of emotions he was feeling for Susanna.

In that mixture, undeniably, lust continued to be uppermost, but the longer he was with her, the more it took on dimensions that were deeper, fuller, richer than any of the many, wild variations of the feelings he had experienced to date. He couldn't remember his heart ever beating as furiously as it did whenever they kissed. Never before had his preoccupation with a woman been so all-consuming. Never had his desire to absorb a woman into his very self been so compelling, nor the primal urge to mate, possess and shield been so intense.

He told himself it was because he'd come to care for this woman as a friend. That was something new. Always before, women *friends* had been and remained just that—friends.

Since his divorce, women who'd become, for lack of a better word, his so-called *girl*friends, had been chosen from a totally different category of female and with a different criterion in mind. Brains, or an aptitude for stimulating conversation, for instance, had never mattered nearly as much as a luscious and willing body.

Some people—most notably his parents and sister—had considered this attitude a lamentable shortcoming on his part, but until quite recently this state of affairs had suited Jeffrey's bachelor style very well. He and his lovers understood and pleasured one another, but didn't try to chain each other down.

Enter Susanna Jaeger, the woman who, with just a few kisses, had shot to hell the practices and conventions of nearly a decade. Not only did he like her tremendously as a friend. He wanted her as a woman in ways he'd never desired one before.

The idea of chaining her down was damnably tempting, and while the notion of *being* chained again himself still gave him an instant case of itchy feet and the jitters, it wasn't nearly as daunting as it had once been.

Already deeply disturbed by those feelings, was it any wonder he'd lain furious, hurt and sleepless all night after he'd realized Susanna intended to split without him?

He hadn't stopped to analyze *how* the knowledge, the certainty, of her plan had come to him. It had, that was all he knew. Call it gut instinct, intuition or mental telepathy—the bottom line was that somewhere in the course of last night's dinner, Susanna's long and heavy silences—broken now and then with uncharacteristically stilted and awkward smatterings of conversation—he had *known*.

And knowing, he had been—and, to be honest, still was—furious. With her for trying to dupe him, and with himself for feeling so damned betrayed.

Frowning fiercely, Jeff opened his eyes long enough to slant a quick, not very friendly glance at his silent seatmate. His heart was instantly softened by what he saw.

Susanna was asleep. Her body had sagged sideways as much as it was able, given the seat belt's restraint, so that the back of her head rested in the junction of seat and window frame. Her hands were folded as if in prayer atop her left thigh. Unruly curls framed her delicate features like a dark halo, and luxurious lashes formed twin crescents of blackness beneath her closed lids.

It was her lips, however, that stirred Jeffrey most. Sensuously full and relaxed in sleep, they curved sweetly in a heart-stopping smile.

Wanting nothing so much as to lean over and kiss her first awake and then senseless, Jeff shakily traced the smile with one finger. The jolt of electrifying reaction he felt when her mouth pursed and the tip of her tongue flicked moistly against his finger, made him jerk his hand away as if stung.

His heart flip-flopped in response to Susanna's soft and husky chuckle. "You're awake," he accused gruffly.

"Only just." She stretched, giving in to a lusty yawn, then gave him an endearingly abashed grin and clapped a hand to her mouth. It was light enough now to see the blush staining her cheeks as she wriggled upright in the seat and tugged at her sweater. "Your touch woke me."

"I'm sorry." Jeffrey was entranced by Susanna's every gesture, and touched by the obvious shyness she was suddenly feeling. "You were smiling in your sleep."

Looking at him, for one beat of her heart, her gaze melded with his.

"I was dreaming," Susanna murmured, her senses reeling, need settled over her like a net, trapping her breath.

"Of your father?" Jeff asked the question, though he knew the answer even before she gave it.

"No," she said. "Not of my father." Her lashes fluttered and her gaze slid to his lips in an unmistakable message.

"Susanna." Jeff gripped her slender hand, almost crushing it, so great was his need to touch her, to hold her, however chastely and for however short a moment in time. "You make me want things I have no right to want from you," he murmured huskily, bringing his face close to hers. "More than holding hands, more than kisses. . . ."

"Oh, Jeffrey." Hungry for greater physical contact and no longer shy now that their mutual desire had been brought into the open, Susanna scooted closer, laid her head against Jeff's shoulder and her hand upon the muscular hardness of his thigh.

For quite a while neither spoke. Jeff was hoping that total concentration on the back of Barney Golding's head would help him overcome the relentless, primitive urges that had him rigid and hurting.

That was why he noticed that every now and then Barney cast quick, increasingly sharp glances into the rearview mirror.

"What's up?" he asked. "Did you spot something?"

"Naw." Barney's frown was fierce. "Go back to sleep."

"I wasn't sleeping."

"Yeah, I noticed." The corners of Barney's eyes in the mirror creased in a grin. "Some guys have all the luck."

Jeff felt himself color, making Barney guffaw. "Say, how about some music to go along with the . . . mood?" he needled, and hooted when Jeff rewarded his humor with a rude gesture.

Jostled, Susanna lifted her head off Jeff's shoulder. Aware that the moment of closeness was past, she straightened and would have removed her hand from Jeff's thigh, had he not clamped down on it and kept it there.

She glanced into his face and was warmed by the quick, intimate smile he gave her. "Stay," he said, as the soft strains of some mellow, golden oldies tune filled the air.

Susanna stayed. After a while she asked, "I never thought, Jeffrey—should I have brought provisions along on this trip?"

"Provisions?"

"Yes." She looked at him earnestly. "You know, food. Now that we are on the *Autobahn*—"

"It's called a freeway here."

"All right, whatever. Freeway. My point is, will there be somewhere to eat?"

Jeff peered at her, grinning. "By any chance would this be your politely backhanded way of saying you're hungry?"

Her cheeks turning pink, Susanna laughed. "Now that you mention it ... I'm starved, actually."

"Well, in that case," Jeff pronounced, "you shall eat. Driver, find us a restaurant. The lady is starving."

"Starvin', huh?" Barney tossed another frowning glance into the mirror and, after a moment, added, "Good a time as any, I guess. Sign says there's a place off o' this exit."

Flipping on the turn signal, he deftly merged right and exited the freeway, still glancing back every second or two with a formidable frown. Moments later, the battered sedan rocked to a halt in the graveled parking lot of a small café. Its sign read, Helen's Home Cookin'. Breakfast Anytime. Barney exploded out of his door, just as a low-slung, black foreign car sped past and disappeared around a bend in the road ahead.

"Damn it all to hell and back!" he roared. "I didn't get a look at the license!" And for quite some time he continued to burn Susanna's ears with the most inventive string of expletives she had ever heard.

At last Jeff said grimly, "All right, Golding. What's going on?"

"Go eat something, Kent."

Jeff ignored that. "We're being tailed, aren't we?"

Susanna looked worriedly from one man to the other. "Tailed?"

They paid her no attention. Still squinting after the vanished black car and furiously chomping on his dead cigar, Barney grunted. "Maybe."

"Damn it, Barn," Jeff flared, "don't give me that. Who are they? Any ideas?"

"Some."

"Mind sharing them with me?"

"With *us*," Susanna put in, determined to be part of the exchange.

"Yeah, I do." Barney's sudden grin held little humor. "But since I know you'll only keep bugging me about it, I'll tell ya." He narrowed his eyes at her. "Word is that you, lady, were followed to this country."

"No!" Susanna clapped a hand to her mouth. "But...but who...?"

"Your father's friends I told you about. Otrovsky and company."

"Otrovsky?" Susanna shook her head. "But I don't even know the man. Or anything about him!"

"Which doesn't mean diddly, since he obviously knows all about you!"

"Susanna." Seeing Susanna's white-faced distress, Jeff put his arm around her shoulder and tucked her protectively against his side. "Who in Berlin knew you were coming to this country?"

She looked at him helplessly. "Why, any number of people, I suppose. I mentioned it to the travel agency, the passport authorities. Even at the hospital where I was employed...."

"Any friends or acquaintances who mighta shot off their mouth?" Barney interjected.

Susanna shook her head. "Not really. I—" She spread her hands with a despairing half shrug. "Look, between work and study and wanting to save all the money I could, I never had much of a social life. Except perhaps... But no."

"What?" Jeff and Barney asked in unison.

"Gerhard and Ilse Meister," Susanna said slowly. "They were friends of my mother and stepfather more than mine, but—" She broke off with another vehement shake of her head. "No. It can't have been them. Why would they possibly wish me ill?"

"Maybe not you, but your father."

"But that amounts to the same thing!" she cried.

"To you, yes." She saw Jeff and Barney exchange glances. "Were they members of the party?"

"Well, yes. Of course."

"Ranking?"

Susanna shrugged again, horrified by the possibility that the kindly couple who had always treated her like a daughter could have misused the trust she'd placed in them.

"Gerhard was. And Ilse worked in the same ministry where my mother used to be employed. Of course, all of this ended when the Wall—"

"Sure," Barney interrupted, "we understand that. Just like we understand that the fact your friends mighta been finks upsets you. Don't let it. Maybe it wasn't them who tipped off Otrovsky and even if it was—what're we gonna do about it? We're being followed, but we kinda expected to be, which is why I'm here, right? Right. So we'll keep our eyes peeled, right? Again right. Meanwhile..."

Rubbing his hands together in a gesture of finality that appeared to signal the end of his interest in the conversation, he forestalled further discussion by saying, "Didn't one o' you mention breakfast?"

Leaving Jeff and Susanna to follow or not, he headed toward the café.

Jeff looked into Susanna's troubled eyes and gave her a reassuring squeeze. "Don't worry about it anymore," he advised her gently. "Like Barney said, it could've been anyone."

"Yes, but—"

"Shh." He dropped a light kiss upon her lips. "Things look a lot brighter on a full stomach. Let's go eat."

Hours later, Susanna, Jeff and Barney were near the town of Roseburg, Oregon. It was only about four in the afternoon, but on a drizzly December day in the Northwest that meant it was almost completely dark. It had been a long and emotionally taxing day.

The morning's tensions, the doubts and renewed surge of fear, had left Susanna drained and depressed. Neither the famous Helen's hearty country breakfast of a three-egg omelet with mounds of hash browns and slices of bacon a quarter inch thick, nor the tar-black brew Helen called coffee, had done very much to restore Susanna. But Jeffrey's questioning glances, as well as his and Barney's touching attempts to divert her, had made her assume a light mood, an effort that had only sapped her more.

She was alone in the back seat but noticed that at regular intervals, Barney would continue to glance sharply into the rearview mirror. And Jeffrey, on the pretext of turning to talk with her, would let his eyes slide past her to the rear window.

"Have either of you seen any more of that car?" she asked, twisting for another look around. "I sure haven't."

"Me, neither," Jeff said, while Barney merely grunted noncommittally, his facial expression sour.

"I say we call it a day," he said after a while. "Keep your eyes open for some signs that say motel."

By the time they neared Roseburg and what they hoped would be a decent hotel where they could crash for the night, they had agreed that the next day they'd leave the busy Interstate behind, make their way to the coast, and follow the much less traveled Highway 101 south to their destination. A tail of any kind would thus be much easier to detect.

"By the way, that's as good a place as any to stay," Jeff said, reading aloud the name of a prestigious, nationally known chain of motor hotels.

"Yeah," Barney grunted feelingly. "Better'n some mom'n pop joint with lots of little cabins tucked away in the woods. I'm too bushed to play cops 'n robbers tonight."

Taking the exit the sign had indicated, and after a short jaunt along yet another frontage road, he braked the car to a stop beneath an imposing, massively pillared portico. Leaving Susanna to gaze admiringly around, he and Jeffrey went into the lobby to register.

They booked two rooms. One—the one Susanna would be using—in the name of Mr. and Mrs. Johnson, and the other—Jeff and Barney's digs—using another fictitious name. No use making it easy for the pursuers, they figured, and as a further precaution paid in cash.

Jeff accepted the room keys, with the desk clerk's good wishes for a pleasant night's stay, and returned to the car. Barney chose to walk to their rooms at the back of the building. Ostensibly to stretch his legs. . . .

Before sliding into the driver's seat, moved by Susanna's tired smile, Jeff gave in to the impulse and, leaning into the back seat, kissed Susanna squarely upon the mouth.

"Hello, Mrs. Johnson," he murmured, following that first quick kiss with a slower, more thorough one. "Your boudoir and a good night's rest are just around the corner." He caressed her cheek. "I only wish I could share them with you."

They kissed again, lingeringly, aware only of each other.

Chapter Eight

Susanna's room number was 127. Jeff and Barney were right next door. A connecting door between the two rooms could be opened, and soon was.

Jeffrey stood in the doorway, getting a kick out of watching Susanna look around. To him the tasteful accoutrements of the room were pretty well standard, but he could see how to Susanna's unspoiled and unsophisticated eye they might be quite impressive. Certainly this room was a far cry from the one he'd "rescued" her from, back in Seattle.

And so he watched her, feeling a mixture of indulgence and tenderness as she wandered around, touching here, trailing a finger in feather-light exploration there. She sat on the queen-size bed, experimentally bounced, then quickly got up and guiltily smoothed the discreetly hued spread she had barely rumpled.

"This is all so . . . so grand," she finally whispered, turning to face Jeffrey at last. "I cannot possibly afford this. . . ."

"And you don't have to," Jeff assured her. "Uncle Sam's footing the bill."

"Uncle Sam?" Susanna repeated, frowning. "Jeffrey, I don't understand. Why would your uncle—?"

"He wouldn't." Jeff grinned in spite of his preoccupation, and because he knew his own uncles well. "All of my uncles are tighter'n a panty girdle on a fat lady, but Uncle *Sam* is different. He's all of us, you see."

Susanna didn't see in the least.

"He's what we call the American government. He's a figure of speech."

Then Susanna understood but, for once, was not entertained by this lesson in the American vernacular. Old habits and ingrained mistrust were slow to die, so she knew that whenever a government was generous, it invariably expected repayment. In terms that were not always pleasant.

"Why would your government be willing to pay for our lodging?" she demanded. "I have nothing and I *know* nothing that could possibly be of interest to them."

"You're Joseph Harrison Miller's daughter," Jeff told her. "And as such they know they owe you. Just as they owe him."

He walked toward her, but didn't reach out and gather her close as he longed to.

"Your father gave his life for his country, Susanna. Oh, I know he's alive, but he carries around indelible scars from the work he did, and he's no longer able to live as the person he came into the world to be. Joseph Harrison Miller is gone as surely as if he *had* died. And imperfect though our country may be, it honors its debts and doesn't forget its heroes. Your father was a hero to the cause of democracy and freedom, Susanna."

Now Jeffrey did touch her. He cupped her shoulders and gently urged her toward him. Susanna didn't resist.

"You're a hero's daughter. This—" He looked around with a jaded expression in his eyes. "This hotel room is paltry recompense indeed for what Harry Miller has given to his country."

He pulled her closer still. His voice grew lower, and roughened with feeling. "Enjoy it, Susanna. You deserve it." He kissed her then, gently, softly, longingly, and whispered, "Relax, sweetheart. Enjoy."

"Oh, Jeffrey..." Inhaling Jeffrey's scent, absorbing his warmth, the steady and reassuring beat of his heart, Susanna wanted nothing so much as to melt into him and let things happen. This man was so good, so kind, this Jeffrey Kent, who had not felt to her like a stranger even aboard that airplane on which—it now seemed eons ago—they had sat side by side, nothing more to each other than chance fellow passengers.

He'd been concerned for her even then, in the casual and thoroughly disarming way she'd come to think of as typically American. They were a warm, generous people, these citizens of her father's country. She loved them and wanted more than anything to be like them. A part of them.

But even more than that... Susanna raised her eyes to Jeff's and smiled. Even more than that she wanted to become a part of Jeffrey Kent.

As their gazes lingered and heated, she watched his eyes widen with dawning understanding and a kind of wonder, and reveled in the knowledge that she thrilled him as he thrilled her. She watched him lower his head and didn't flinch. His lips were close now, his intention clear. She leaned into him and welcomed both.

"Ahem..."

They sprang apart as guiltily as a pair of necking adolescents caught by the school principal, to see Barney standing in the open doorway, eyeing them quizzically.

"Pardon me all to hell," he said wryly, "but could you guys lay off each other long enough to maybe talk about food?"

"Food?" His head still reeling, Jeff's brain was slow to kick into gear.

"Yeah. As in dinner."

"Oh." Grinning, his equilibrium restored, Jeff released Susanna who self-consciously smoothed her hair and refused to meet Barney's gaze. "That kind of food."

"Bright boy." Barney chomped on his cigar. "Wanna eat in or out?"

"I don't know." Food not being a high priority item just at the moment, Jeff didn't much care either way. "Susanna? Shall we do room service?"

"Will they have nachos?"

"Nachos?" Barney looked appalled. "For dinner?"

Jeff grinned. "Susanna's become a junk-food junkie," he explained. "In spite of the fact that she never misses an opportunity to lecture *me* on proper nutrition...."

In the end they opted to eat outside the room, doing so in the hotel coffee shop. The meal was mediocre and, tired after the long day, they immediately afterward returned to their rooms and called it a night.

The next morning they got an early start, anxious to be on their way. After a quick breakfast, they lost no time readying the few items they had unpacked and stowing them in the car.

"I'm glad we decided to head toward 101," Jeff remarked to Susanna. He slammed down the lid of the trunk and slid in behind the wheel. Barney had announced a need for more sleep and, with orders not to bother him, had parked himself in the back seat. "The coast tends to get fogged in by late afternoon, this time of year, but we'll have found a place to stay before it gets too thick."

"And meantime we can see if we're being followed," Susanna said.

"That's the general idea."

The ninety-odd-mile drive from just out of Roseburg to Coos Bay would have taken less than two hours by the highway. This road, however, serpentined its way through some spectacular, wooded countryside, and so it took them close to four hours. But they didn't regret having chosen this route, and Susanna, particularly, couldn't exclaim often enough at the beauty of the land and the majesty of the old-growth timber.

Jeff told her about the redwood forest that they would drive through the next day, but Susanna found it difficult to believe that the sequoias he spoke of could grow even bigger and taller than the giant conifers she was seeing today.

It was quite dark and so foggy they'd been forced to creep the last few miles at a walking pace, by the time they pulled in at the quaint little collection of cabins called the Sea Star Motel. Not very far south of Coos Bay, where they'd found no vacancies, it was located in a town called Beecham. The sign in front proudly announced they had color TV plus kitchenettes, and that water beds were available, too.

Susanna was decidedly leery about the latter. "I'd get seasick," she told Jeff, and didn't mind a bit when he teasingly dubbed her a stick-in-the-mud.

Going in to register, they learned that only one cabin was available. Since the only alternative to staying at the Sea Star would be to keep driving farther up the highway in the dark and the fog to the next bigger town—an idea that didn't much appeal to any of them—they decided they could make do here.

Jeff once again registered Susanna and himself as Mr. and Mrs. Johnson, and got a bang out of making a great show of putting his arm around Susanna's waist, calling her "honey" like a real husband.

The genial elderly manager—Abe Prescott by name—told them that there was a good restaurant not far up the road, and free instant coffee or tea in their cabin, which was #2.

They parked in front of the cabin's rickety porch and lugged their stuff inside. Looking around, Jeff commented that the furnishings leaned toward early rummage sale, with the dreary colors to match, and ended up having to explain to Susanna what he meant by that.

The much-lauded kitchenette consisted of a hot plate at one end of a chrome-and-Formica table fronted by two unmatched chairs, a minuscule refrigerator beneath a sink and counter arrangement that housed one dented pot, a blackened frying pan, a few place settings of unbreakable dishes and utensils.

Susanna inspected each item with great interest and announced that she could well envision spending a cozy vacation here. Barney, fiddling with the color TV and finding that they didn't have cable, merely snorted in disgust, impatiently snapped the thing off and went to inspect the bathroom.

Emerging a minute later, he brought up the subject of the one piece of furniture they had all so far neither discussed nor inspected—the bed. There was only one. Not king-size or even queen. It was, quite simply, a plain old garden-variety standard double.

"You and Susanna go ahead and share this thing," Barney said, bending to squeeze the skinny mattress and pulling a face as he straightened. "My back's already shot, so I might as well curl up in *that*."

He indicated the room's single, lumpy and decidedly uninviting stuffed easy chair.

"But, Barney," Jeff began to protest.

Susanna exclaimed, "But that's awful!"

Barney silenced them both. "You got a better idea?" he growled. "Like maybe all three of us should get on the bed? Or maybe you oughta take the chair, Kent, and I get to sleep with the lady? Or how about *she* takes the chair?"

He plunked himself into "his" chair, glowering. "Come off it, will ya!"

The issue thus settled, it was dropped as a topic of conversation, but stuck in Jeff's mind. So, all right, maybe stretching out side by side on a bed, fully clothed and with a live-in chaperon wasn't exactly the stuff steamy seduction scenes were made of, but it would still be a facsimile of the kind of intimacy he longed to share with Susanna.

Taking his turn in the bathroom, to wash his hands and smooth his hair, Jeffrey chuckled at the feverish way he was looking forward to spending the night with a completely dressed woman in his arms. *Maybe* in his arms, he amended. And not just any woman; one woman. *Susanna.*

Somewhere, somehow, Susanna had ceased to be merely a woman to him. She had become special, more special than he would ever have thought possible. She had become a friend. Not that he didn't desire her—the aching tightness in his loins was palpable testimony to the fact that he did—but he was drawn to her on so many other levels, as well.

He admired her courage, her spunk. Her capacity for love and—more and more—for laughter, despite the hardships she'd endured. He enjoyed her unspoiled freshness. She was special. What he felt for her was special.

Looking at his reflection in the mirror, Jeff nodded with something like fatalistic acceptance, quite certain now. What he felt for Susanna Jaeger was—

"Jeffrey!" Susanna was knocking gently on the bathroom door. "Darling, Mr. Prescott is here to ask if there's anything we need because he'll be closing the office for the night.''

Darling.

That one word was the only thing Jeff heard. He very much liked the sound of it coming from Susanna, with just a hint of a foreign accent. A man could get used to hearing the word said just like that by the woman he—

The word was there again, right on the tip of his tongue. But though it took an effort, Jeff quickly swallowed it and put another, less daunting one in its place.

The woman he *liked* as much as he liked Susanna Jaeger.

Straightening, he ruthlessly squelched the little voice that was calling him a coward. ''Where's Barney?'' he asked.

''He stepped out for a moment.''

''Okay, then. I'll be right out.''

''Hi, Abe,'' he said cordially minutes later, coming out of the bathroom and draping an arm around Susanna's shoulders in a husbandly gesture. ''It's very good of you to ask, but offhand I can't think of a thing we might need.''

Except for another cabin for Barney Golding.

Casting a fond glance at Susanna's suddenly flushed face, he added, ''The wife and I plan to grab a bite to eat at that restaurant you mentioned, and then we'll be ready to . . .''

His gaze dropped to Susanna's lips, softly parted, and stayed there. '' . . . call it a night.''

"Well, that's just fine, then. Just fine," the manager said, backing out of the cabin. "The place stops serving at eight, by the way, just so's you folks know."

"Thanks." Chuckling quietly, Jeff closed the door behind their host. Since one of his arms was already around Susanna, it seemed only right to put the other around her, too.

"So," he said, lowering his head until their lips were only a fraction of an inch apart and their gazes were melting into each other, "tell me, dear wife. Are you hungry?"

"Famished." Susanna's voice was barely audible. Jeff uttered a groan, then his mouth on hers stole her breath.

"This is starting to get old, people," Barney said, noisily reentering the cabin. He shook his head, chuckling when they moved apart and exchanged a pained glance. "I can see it's just as well I decided to nose around a bit and not go with you guys for dinner."

Jeff and Susanna's protests were token, at best, and Barney's wry expression told them he knew it.

"It could, o' course, be nothin' more'n an overdeveloped sense of distrust and suspicion on my part," he told them, his habitually aggrieved facial expression taking on a few additional creases, "but damned if I can shake the feeling that something's not right, that somebody's out there. . . ."

"Really?" Jeff frowned. "In that case, maybe we ought to stick with you. . . ."

"And do what?"

Jeff shrugged. "You tell me. You're the expert—"

"Right." Barney waved them toward the door. "So here's what I'm tellin' you. Go eat. And keep your eyes peeled."

The Crab 'n' Slab restaurant their landlord had so enthusiastically touted was a roundish structure, shaped to resemble a Dungeness crab. It perched on a knoll overlooking the sea.

At least it was supposed to.

Jeffrey and Susanna, from their table in front of the semicircular wall of windows, had no way of knowing for sure. An impenetrable, gray curtain of fog obscured everything but a few tufts of the beach grass that grew close to the building.

But then, chances were that even on a crystal-clear midsummer night they wouldn't have had eyes for the view.

Jeff and Susanna were fully occupied by, and completely content with, gazing only at each other. The room, though fairly bustling with diners and redolent with a vast potpourri of surf 'n' turf smells, could have been empty for all the notice they took of their surroundings.

Though Susanna had earlier professed to be hungry, and actually had been, she had only picked at her salad and was now putting a similar effort into the grilled salmon steak she'd ordered on the waiter's, and Jeffrey's, recommendation.

Jeff's excellent steak and crab special might have been lumpfish and shoe leather, he wouldn't have noticed the difference. He had eyes only for Susanna, and his appetite was equally concentrated away from his plate.

"How's everything?" the waiter asked genially, deftly refilling their wineglasses.

"Just great, thanks."

"Delicious."

Neither looked up at the man as they answered, causing the waiter to say, "Aha," with a knowing tone. "Anything else I can get you folks?"

"Not right now, thanks," Jeff replied.

Alone again, he raised his glass. "A toast. What shall we drink to? Us?"

"Us?" Susanna queried softly, quizzically arching a brow.

"Sure. Why not? We're friends, aren't we? On top of which—" Jeff wiggled his brows in a comic leer "—aren't we about to sleep together?"

The way that sounded. Though she knew Jeff was teasing her, Susanna felt her pulse leap and her face grow heated. "Yes, we are."

"Well, then..." Jeff touched the rim of his glass to her. "Here's to us."

"To us."

They sipped. Susanna saw Jeff watch hungrily as she put out the tip of her tongue to retrieve an errant drop of the tart chardonnay. His gaze left no doubt that he would gladly have done the honors.

Because she would just as gladly have let him, and because she suddenly felt shy about letting Jeffrey read in her eyes the depth of her desire for him, Susanna gave the act of setting down her glass her complete attention.

"The wine is lovely," she said, after clearing her throat, which had become constricted with emotion. "California, you say?"

"Napa, yes." Jeffrey, too, put down his glass. "A beautiful valley not far from San Francisco. At another time, in different circumstances, I would have loved to show it to you."

"And I would have liked that. Another time."

They fell silent, then Susanna said wistfully, "Will there be another time for us, Jeffrey, do you suppose?"

"I'd like there to be."

"So would I."

"Then we'll plan on it."

"Yes." She looked into her glass, then back at him. "I, ah, I suppose it would have to be after your next assignment sometime, wouldn't it?"

"I s'pose." Jeff frowned. A vague sense of something like self-annoyance darkened his mood. The thought of another assignment, of spending yet another six, eight or twelve months, in one of the world's trouble spots, enduring the Lord knows what deprivations, dangers and health hazards for no other reason than the edification of an uncaring public back home, filled him with a never-before experienced distaste. Always before he had craved that kind of thing. When had it stopped? And why?

He was very much afraid that the answer to that last question was, literally, looking him in the face. So Jeff's tone was tinged with impatience when he added, "It's not like either of us has time before then, is it?"

Susanna watched her thumb and forefinger gently twirl the wineglass. "No," she said, without looking up. "Of course it's not." After another pause she asked, "When do you go? On your next assignment, I mean."

"Pretty well right after New Year's."

"Where?" She spoke very softly.

Jeff shrugged, frowning more darkly at the glass he, too, had begun to twist this way and that. "Nothing's concrete yet, but it'll probably be the Middle East again. There's a lot of news there still...."

"A lot of danger, too."

Hearing Susanna's tone, vibrant with concern, Jeff directed his frown toward her. "There's danger everywhere, Susanna. Just being alive is dangerous—"

"But not fatal."

"Oh, yeah?" Jeff knew very well it was sheer contrariness brought on by his own sudden aversion to the job he used to love that made him add flippantly, "Ever heard of anyone leaving this earth alive, sweetheart?"

"Don't," Susanna said sharply. "This is not funny. I care what happens to you and—"

"Susanna." Jeff reached across the table, caught her hand and cradled it in his . "I'm sorry." He looked into her dark, troubled eyes and bit his lip. "Look, nothing's going to happen to me. All right?"

"No. Not all right." She looked away. "I couldn't bear it if—"

"Why?" He tugged at her hand until she turned her unhappy face toward him. "Why, Susanna?" he repeated. "Tell me."

"Because—" The intensity of Jeff's gaze made it impossible for Susanna to look away. "Because—"

I love you. She moistened dry lips and struggled to keep what was in her heart from showing in her eyes.

"Because I can't afford to lose any more people I...I care about," she finished softly.

Slowly, gently, Jeff lifted the hand he still held and brought it to his lips. "I care about you, too," he said with tenderness and conviction. But just as soon as the words were out, they seemed utterly inadequate. Still, to say more . . .

He sighed, feeling a familiar sense of depression settle over him like the thick Pacific coast fog. Before the sensation could take hold and ruin what had begun as such a promising evening, he forced a brisk tone and a smile.

"Come on." Taking Susanna's hand, he pulled her to her feet. "I don't think you feel like eating any more than I do. Let's go home."

The startled glance they exchanged at the word *home*, lengthened into a look of sizzling awareness that kept them riveted for several accelerated heartbeats. They were standing body to body, Susanna's delicate, yet strong fingers in the clasp of Jeffrey's warm, much larger hand. Their lips were only inches apart, parted and moving closer.

"Excuse me, folks." The waiter's dry apology, accompanied by the pungent aroma of two steaming buckets of clams balanced aloft in close proximity, reminded them that they were blocking the aisle of a public restaurant. Susanna moved aside with a breathless little laugh.

Jeff's chuckle was both rueful and self-deprecatory; he, too, made room for the waiter to pass. They walked one behind the other toward the exit. Jeff paid the bill, helped Susanna into her raincoat and then, hand in hand, they left the restaurant.

Outside, the fog was almost tangible, at once eerie and comforting. It enfolded Jeffrey and Susanna in a soft, clammy embrace and lent an air of mysterious unreality to such mundane items as lampposts, trees and the upended, weathered hulls of several rowboats.

Gravel crunched beneath their feet. In the distance, at regular intervals, a fog horn moaned its warning to ships at sea.

It had gotten colder and, quite naturally, Jeff put his arm around Susanna and tucked her against his side. They had come the quarter mile or so from the motel on foot, walking briskly, glad of the fresh air and exercise. Barney, in spite of the niggling sense of unease he'd alluded to, had said to go for it.

Now, though, aware that these precious moments of privacy were almost over, they were loath to reach the motel. They dawdled, stopping often to exchange a kiss, a lingering touch.

All too soon to suit them, they turned into the driveway leading to their cabin. "I want you to know something, Susanna," Jeff said. "For what it's worth, if circumstances were different, if *I* were different, you'd be the woman I'd most want to make a life with."

"Thank you, Jeffrey."

But Jeff didn't want to be thanked. He wanted to be challenged, argued with, so that he could defend his position. Since she didn't argue, he defended himself, anyway.

"Damn it, Susanna, you don't understand."

"I do."

"I mean, I didn't get to be the way I am out of the blue, you know."

"Of course you didn't."

"I've got damn good reason to feel the way I do."

"I'm sure you have. Jeffrey..." She stopped walking and, bathed in the dim, muted glow of an overhead yard lamp, turned toward him. She looked into his eyes. "Please," she said. "Don't talk anymore. Don't say anything else. Don't try to explain or rationalize. Let's just accept—" her voice quivered "—the fact that this is how it *is*. While what we feel for each other is strong and, and *special*, there can be nothing between us beyond this." She managed to smile. "Beyond now. We have come together with differing agendas, but the time I've had with you has been magic for me."

"For me, too."

Susanna nodded, accepting that. Pressing her lips together to keep them from trembling, struggling to curve them into another smile, she swallowed painfully. "Let's let it be enough then, Jeffrey."

"But—"

"No." She laid a finger over his mouth and smiled sadly. "No more buts."

Jeff dipped his head without a word and Susanna, her eyes on his, rose on tiptoe to welcome his kiss.

Still embracing, almost oblivious to their surroundings, they were caught in a high beam's twin glare, and then it was dark again as the purr of a high-speed engine faded away.

Chapter Nine

Jeff awoke to the smell of coffee, and opened his eyes to a sight of such tranquil domesticity, it set his teeth on edge.

Susanna, wearing a robe and with a towel wrapped around her head, was sitting at the rickety table, chatting intimately over morning coffee with a damp-haired Barney Golding wearing nothing but jeans and a red-haired bare chest.

Mr. and Mrs. America.

Jealousy, ugly, green and bitter, rose like bile into Jeff's mouth. Damn it, that's *my* woman you're horning in on, Golding, he thought.

After that he might even have given in to the urge to leap off the bed and haul Barney away from that table, had not another voice inside him jeered, *Your* woman, Kent? How do you figure that, old bud?

Defeated by his own conscience, Jeff subsided onto the pillow from which he'd half lifted his head. Still weary, he closed his eyes again. He hadn't slept much that past night, having been excruciatingly aware of the slender woman who had nestled against him in sleep. He hadn't had the willpower to remove her hand from the intimate spot against which it had chosen to rest.

Feeling her there had been torture, but it had been a bit of heaven, too. For a little while it had allowed him to imagine that Susanna was his and he was hers, and that they were free to take these kinds of liberties with each other's bodies anytime they wanted.

And, boy, had he wanted. Did he still!

Jeff clenched his teeth. Damn Barney Golding! If he hadn't horned in on this trip, Susanna might by now be—no, *would have been*—his! Traveling together and wanting each other the way they did, they would inevitably have made love every night of this journey.

Then he thought, Whoa there, old son. You're forgetting a few very pertinent facts here, aren't you? Like the fact that you're supposed to be a globetrotter, a freewheeling Gypsy. Even if it was by inclination more than by profession.

You're a traveling man, Kent—remember that. Home and hearth, bud—they're not for you.

Just as anything less is not for Susanna.

Right.

Except . . . when Jeff opened his eyes again, just a crack, and let them rest on that cozy tableau, when he drank in Susanna's morning-fresh loveliness and felt his body still vibrating from the feel of her in the night, he was no longer sure about those damn facts of his. Or about possibles and impossibles, either.

Bone weary and down in the dumps, eyelids too heavy to keep them aloft any longer, Jeff let himself drift into a fitful snooze full of gore and mayhem, and then, going deeper, slept.

Across the room and outwardly serene, Susanna's emotions, too, were in turmoil. She should have been happy, elated, knowing the end of her journey was near and that as soon as her two companions had seen her safely to her destination, her father's well-being would no longer be in jeopardy. At least, not on her account. In just a little more than a day all her dreams would at last have come true. She would finally be united with the man she had dreamed about, loved and longed for all her life.

Yet she wasn't happy. Not unreservedly, anyway. Tendrils of sadness wound themselves around every one of her happy thoughts because the man she now dreamed about, loved and longed for was Jeffrey Kent. And he was as much, or more, out of reach than her father had ever been.

In her search for Joseph Harrison Miller there had been hope. In her love for Jeffrey Kent there was none.

After tomorrow, or, at most, another day or two beyond that, he would be gone from her life. And with the New Year just ahead, he would be out of the country. He would once again be roaming the world in search of adventures more alluring than any Susanna could ever hope to offer.

Aware that Barney had spoken and was looking at her, waiting for a reply, Susanna shook off the depression that threatened to blacken the first sun-bright day they'd had on this trip. She hadn't come to America for love and romance, she reminded herself, she had come in pursuit of happiness—a life with her father as well as one of simple freedom. With both of those goals nearly attained, how dare she complain?

"I'm sorry." She slanted Barney a rueful smile. "I . . . My mind was elsewhere. I didn't hear what you said."

"Never mind." She saw Barney eye her shrewdly, which made her wonder if the substance of her musings had been readable in her face. But Barney's tone was offhand when he added, rising, "Think I'll get your lover boy there up and at 'em. It's getting late."

"Jeffrey's not my—" *lover boy,* she'd intended to say, but Barney cut her off.

"Just a figure of speech, kid. Don't sweat it. Hey, Kent—" He yanked the covers off Jeff's recumbent, jeans-and-T-shirt-clad form and slapped his naked foot. "Wakey, wakey, sleeping beauty. Hit the deck, we gotta get going!"

Cursing, Jeff struggled out of the bottomless black pit of exhaustion into which he had fallen. Nostrils assailed once again by the smell of coffee, he forced his eyes open and met Susanna's smile. His own lips half curved in response without conscious direction from his brain. Seeing the mug she was holding out to him, he levered himself into a sitting position.

"Damn," he muttered. He was never at his best upon awakening, but felt positively evil on this particular morning. "You're a royal pain, Golding. Anybody ever tell you that?"

"You're getting old and crotchety, Kent," Barney needled, clearly unmoved by the sorry picture his friend presented. "Sure you're up to another assignment overseas?"

Jeff's response was a thunderous glare; he'd been asking himself the very same question.

"I wouldn't talk, bud," he said sourly, managing only a slightly more gracious, "Thanks," when he took the mug of coffee out of Susanna's hands.

Their fingers brushed, and the sizzling shower of sparks the touch ignited along Jeff's nerve ends caused his gaze to snap up to hers and stay there. He couldn't have looked away even if he'd wanted to, not when there was such a world of feeling to be discovered in the velvety darkness of Susanna's incredible eyes. No woman had ever looked at him like that, with such hunger, such intensity, such wistful longing and tenderness. Why, it was almost as if she—

No. Even as the unthinkable word—*love*—dropped like a bomb into Jeff's consciousness, Susanna was already stepping away from the bed. The moment might never have been.

Telling himself he was getting fanciful in his old age, Jeff took a sip of coffee and, raking Susanna's shapely, robe-clad form with a playfully exaggerated leer, forced a light tone. "Lady, if you're this establishment's room service, I can see why the place is so popular."

"Will you stop being cute, Kent," Barney demanded impatiently, "and get in the bathroom?" Fully dressed now, right down to the raincoat and ever-present cigar, he planted himself at the foot of the bed. "It's practically noon. You got ten minutes."

"It's 8:00 a.m. and I only need five." Jeff was already halfway to the bathroom.

"Take ten and finish your coffee. We're not stopping till lunch. If then." Barney turned to Susanna. "I'm gonna nose around a bit outside and bring the car out front. Bring your gear out as soon as you're dressed."

A few minutes later they were under way, heading back to the freeway on Barney's say-so. Having spotted no tail the previous day in spite of their constant vigilance, he insisted they'd make much better time on the interstate. All of a sudden, time was of the essence. He had an overload of work waiting for him back in Seattle, he informed them. Besides which he'd had about all he could stomach of playing nursemaid to a pair of lovesick fools making cow eyes and kissy-kissy. He couldn't spare this clambake an hour longer than absolutely necessary.

But when Jeff very mildly suggested that he leave them to make their own way south, as they'd originally planned, Barney wouldn't hear of it.

"And leave you in charge?" he heckled. "I wouldn't be able to sleep nights, worrying...."

Lunch was late and eaten on the run. Some heartburn-causing fast food washed down by California orange juice. They were *in* California now, the men informed Susanna, and chuckled when she wondered where the palm trees were.

After the hard day's drive, they spent the night in a nondescript motel just off the freeway, somewhere in the vicinity of Sacramento and Susanna saw palm trees at last. She stood transfixed beneath a slightly scruffy one, hands clasped to her bosom and eyes closed.

"Listen," she whispered as the wind rustled the dry palm fronds. "Isn't it wonderful?"

Hard-boiled though both men claimed to be, they were touched enough by Susanna's simple pleasure that they did as she asked and silently stood beside her, listening.

As they had back in Roseburg, Jeff and Barney shared one room and Susanna was given another. They called it a night after eating yet another fast-food meal. After that, though dead tired, Susanna spent seemingly endless hours awake, tossing on her solitary bed.

Could one night spent curled up next to Jeffrey Kent's warm body *really* have spoiled her for sleeping alone? she wondered dismally. If so, she was in even deeper trouble than she'd already suspected. And she'd have many a lonely, sleepless night to look forward to.

Near dawn, her arms firmly embracing the extra pillow, Susanna finally drifted into a fitful sleep. Consequently, she was more than a little out of sorts when the telephone woke her what seemed like only seconds later.

Nor did the fact that it was Jeff's voice on the other end improve her mood. Quite the contrary. Laying the blame for her heartache squarely on him, she snapped, "If you even dare to say something cute and American like 'Up and at 'em,' I swear, I'll hang up on you."

And did so, forcefully, when laughter was Jeff's only reply.

Her mood didn't improve until they had wound their way through the Santa Susana Mountains and down into the San Fernando Valley. "How delightful. An entire mountain range bearing my name. I think it's a good omen, don't you?"

Taking Santa Monica Boulevard off I-405, they headed toward West Hollywood and, suddenly, they were there.

Joseph Harrison Miller's house struck Susanna as something out of one of those rare Hollywood films that had occasionally found their way across the Berlin Wall and that she, on even rarer occasions, had spent the money to see: whitewashed stucco walls, their starkness relieved by irregular patches of exposed red brick; a profusion of colorful and exotic flora, and gracefully arched entrances. The sum of all these features, in Susanna's opinion, amounted to the perfect image of a Spanish hacienda.

Fragrant air and mellow temperatures, palm trees swaying in the gentle breeze, their fronds rustling, completed the illusion of having entered a fairy world, a dream.

Her dream. And now, finally, her reality. This splendid mansion was her father's house. Her father's *home*.

Would it, could it, become hers, as well?

Driving through the huge, wrought iron gates that had opened as if by magic after Barney, at the wheel, had disclosed their names to the disembodied voice coming from a box on a post, Susanna was suddenly seized by panic. The place their car was winding its way toward along the wide, curving driveway, was so grand, so imposing. So intimidating.

What kind of man lived in a house like this? Who *was* this man, her father? What did she really know of him, other than the fact that he had once loved her mother and had been loved by her in return?

Recalling that, Susanna was reassured. Her mother had loved this man. What else did she really need to know? Could her mother have given her heart to any but the very best of men? No. Never.

All at once she relaxed. She glanced gratefully at the men in the front seat. She knew they'd been tactfully silent to give her a chance to prepare herself for the meeting ahead. Her gaze touched on the russet hair that curled along the edge of Jeffrey's collar, and went on to linger on his half-averted profile. The proud sweep of his nose, the curve of his lips above that strong, stubborn chin. How dear he was.

She touched his shoulder and met the somber gaze he turned toward her with a tremulous smile. "It'll be all right," she said softly, wishing away the little catch in her voice. She knew it wasn't there because she was afraid, but because the unspoken love she felt for this man was so strong. "Won't it, Jeffrey?"

Jeff briefly covered her hand with his. "Of course it will." Giving her a reassuring smile, he faced forward again. "Just look," he said, pointing, "there's an entire committee lined up to welcome you."

Eager for the dream to finally become reality, Susanna was out of the car before Barney had even turned off the engine. She hesitated only briefly, and then ran toward the small group assembled beneath the spacious, bougainvillea-draped portico.

She was already halfway there when all hell broke loose. The group of people she'd been approaching exploded into frenzied action.

There was shouting, then she heard Jeffrey's voice. "Get down, Susanna! Down!"

For an instant, bewildered, she couldn't respond, but froze where she stood. And then she felt herself lifted, carried a few steps at a fast clip and dumped like a rag doll into a clump of shrubbery.

"Stay there," a deep voice, not Jeffrey's, commanded. "Don't you dare move."

She didn't, except to inch her head upward until she could see. The scene her horrified gaze encountered made her blood run cold. Another car was parked behind Barney's old wreck, a silver one, obviously expensive. Men were fighting, five of them. Six? Locked into clumps of combat, it was difficult to tell. Grunting and cursing, some rolled on the ground in a tangle of flailing limbs, while others were trading vicious punches.

Where was Jeffrey?

Frantic, her eyes searched for him. There. There he was, but...*Gott im Himmel!*

He was engaged in a macabre dance of violence with another man, shorter, stockier. One pair of arms was aloft, above their heads. And there was a gun. They were struggling over the gun, the gun held by...whom?

Forgetting herself, forgetting safety, Susanna jumped up and craned her neck for a better view. Was that Jeffrey's hand holding the gun? No.

Spitting fire, the weapon discharged with a sharp crack. Susanna screamed. And running, screamed again, when she saw another man violently shove Barney aside to level his gun at Jeff's back.

Her frantic, "Jeffrey! Look out!" coincided with yet another gunshot.

Afterward she was sure her warning had gone unheard, that she'd been too late. Right now, however, she could neither swear nor think as she ran, screaming Jeff's name over and over, toward the man she loved.

She launched herself like a human missile at Jeff's ambusher, then heard another shot....

Coming to was painful. Susanna's head throbbed and her eyelids seemed weighted with lead. She decided to keep them lowered a little while longer. Shifting, she became aware of the hardness of her pillow. Pillow?

Blindly reaching out, she touched a ... face.

"Jeffrey!" Susanna surged upright, only to be gently pressed down again upon the thigh her head had been resting on.

"Right here." He smoothed her hair with a hand that shook. "I'm right here, sweetheart."

"Thank God." Tears gushed as she gripped his hand and held on for dear life. "Thank God."

He was alive. For a moment, Susanna allowed herself to relax. She closed her eyes again. "My head hurts."

"I'm sorry." Another voice, not Jeffrey's. "I'm afraid I didn't have time to be gentle. Either time."

Susanna opened her eyes again and another face swam into view. Round, flushed. Apologetic.

"You tossed me into the bushes?"

"'Fraid so."

"And later?"

"Yup." A rueful shrug. "That was me, too."

Susanna studied the florid features beneath a pate that was as bald and shiny as a lacquered egg. "Who—?"

"Ross Cunningham. I work for your father."

Her father. *Gott im Himmel!* Everything came back to her in a rush. The fighting, the gunshots...

Frantic once more, Susanna struggled to sit up, but Jeff held her back.

"My father!" she gasped, clutching at his jacket. "Did they—?"

"He's fine." Cunningham again. "They never got to him."

"They...?"

"Later, Susanna," Jeff said firmly. "The story-telling will keep. Right now, if you're up to it, I want to get you up on your feet and into the house. Your father is most anxious to see you."

"And I, him." Stifling a moan she managed to stand with Jeff's help. Dizzy, she relied on Jeffrey's strength for a moment and, thankful for his support, raised her face to his with a weak smile. It was instantly replaced by a look of dismay. "Your eye!" she exclaimed. "Oh, Jeffrey..."

"Just a little shiner," Jeff said, resorting to gallows humor in an effort to diffuse her concern. "You should see the other guy."

"No kidding." This from Cunningham. "He's dead."

"Hey, Cunningham!" Barney's voice. Until now, Susanna was ashamed to admit, she hadn't even spared him a thought. "Get your butt over here and let's go. They're waitin' for us downtown...."

"Coming." Cunningham trotted off, tossing a two-fingered salute at Jeff, who was guiding Susanna gently but firmly toward the house.

She stopped walking. "Where are they going?"

"'To take care of the legalities.'" He urged her forward. "Your father's compound was invaded. A man's been killed...."

She turned her head to ask him the obvious question and Jeffrey nodded. "Yes," he said quietly. "Otrovsky."

"And I brought him here." Stopping again, ignoring a renewed surge of dizziness and nausea, Susanna pulled out of Jeff's hold to cover her face. "All this is my fault. I should never have come...."

"No, child. Never say that."

At the sound of the deep, resonant voice behind her, Susanna dropped her hands and whirled, groping for Jeff; another wave of vertigo nearly felled her. "F-father?"

He was in a wheelchair. It took a moment for the realization to penetrate Susanna's rattled brain. His hair was white. All white, and the years had not been kind to him. Beneath that shock of white hair, heavy brows shaded eyes that were infinitely dark. Infinitely sad.

He no longer looked anything at all like the snapshot in the golden heart locket, yet she would have known him anywhere.

Choking back a sob, Susanna was at his side beneath the portico of his great house, on her knees and holding his hand.

A tear rolled unheeded down Harry Miller's deeply lined cheek. Eyes haunted by memories drank in Susanna's features.

He studied her minutely, as if memorizing every feature or mentally comparing them to others, equally well loved.

Susanna regarded him with matching intensity, and when their eyes met, she returned his tender smile.

"Father," she said, her voice shaking with the force of her emotions. Then she was in his arms, sobbing. His hand came down to rest gently on the crown of her head as if in benediction.

At last, Harry Miller looked beyond her to the man who had brought his daughter home. Jeffrey had been keeping a respectful distance, allowing father and daughter the privacy the moment warranted.

"Thank you," Miller said in a voice roughened with feeling. "I thank you from the bottom of my heart."

"Well," Harry Miller said some time later, when he, Susanna and Jeffrey were in the mansion's kitchen, where Prudence Meyer, his cook-housekeeper was plying them with coffee. "What is it they say? All's well that ends well?"

"Yeah." Jeff laughed, though with one lip split by a well-aimed punch on the mouth, it hurt to do so. "I'm sure that's true, though Barney and Cunningham—"

"Ross, yes. My bodyguard."

"Yes." Jeff set down his cup. "Well, he and Barney might not feel that way for a bit."

"*Pshaw.*" Miller dismissed the notion with a negligent wave of the hand. "Like me, Ross has had a lot worse than that flesh wound dished out to him in the course of our long and checkered association. And I'm sure that's not the first broken nose Detective Golding ever sustained, either."

"Hardly." Nursing bruised knuckles, Jeff's chuckle of agreement was dry.

"The main thing is—" Miller caught Susanna's hand and held it in both of his "—that you're unhurt, my Susanna." He looked at her closely and frowned. "You *are* all right, aren't you, child? You're awfully pale."

Susanna shook her head, trying for a smile. "It's nothing," she said feebly. "Just everything catching up with me, I suppose. There was so much chaos, suddenly—"

"I'll say." This from Jeff. "For a moment there, I thought it was going to be all over for me."

Susanna stared at him, remembering, and said softly, "So did I." After a moment she added, "Why wasn't it?"

Nonplussed, Jeffrey stared back at her. "What?"

"Why aren't you dead?"

Not sure how to react to Susanna's uncharacteristically bald question, Jeff began to laugh. "You sound disappointed," he quipped. "And here I've been thinking you saved my life because you cared."

Looking into her eyes, seeing the remembered terror there, his laughter fled abruptly.

"Susanna." He caught her hand and held her gaze; the events of the night were there again between them. The struggle for the gun, Susanna's terror, Jeffrey's sweat. The shot.

And woven through the recollection was every one of the convoluted and unresolved feelings that had been making them so miserable, so . . . happy.

Susanna's eyes once again brimmed with tears; she clumsily got to her feet. "Father, I'd really like to go and lie down now, if you don't mind."

"Of course, my dear." As Jeffrey stood up, Harry Miller rolled to the kitchen door to open it for his daughter. "Have a good rest."

Susanna looked back at Jeffrey. "Will I see you tomorrow morning?"

He smiled. "Count on it."

Susanna didn't get to see Jeffrey until late the following afternoon. It seemed he and Barney, along with her father's nurse-companion and bodyguard, Ross Cunningham, had a lot of unfinished business with the authorities to attend to.

Drained by the events of the previous day and all the tension-filled days before that, Susanna took her father's advice and slept long into the morning, then took a leisurely bath.

Coming down well after the lunch hour, rested and in a much more optimistic frame of mind, she was disappointed to learn that her father and several government agents were sequestered in the library for lengthy talks, making him unavailable for even a greeting. A stroll through the mansion's extensive grounds buoyed her spirits, however. As she had when she first saw the place, she felt transported into another world.

The fact that this would from now on be home seemed scarcely believable.

Several hours later, everybody returned to the house and assembled in the mansion's spacious and airy living room. Susanna felt better. Jeffrey was here, and though she knew it was foolish, with him nearby she felt able to cope with anything.

"A toast," said her father, waiting until they had all raised their delicate flutes of champagne. His eyes resting lovingly on Susanna, he added, "To Maria, the woman I loved who gave me you."

Solemnly they drank. Then, with a laugh that was both youthful and vibrant with joy, the old man threw his glass into the fireplace, where it splintered musically into a hundred sparkling pieces.

"I've always wanted to do that," he said with obvious relish, "but until now there's never been an occasion worthy of the gesture. Please."

He gestured, inviting the others to follow suit and, after a moment's hesitation and some self-conscious laughter, they did. Then the old man drew a flat velvet box out of his jacket pocket, snapped it open and took out the delicate chain with the golden heart he had given Susanna's mother years ago.

"Here, Susanna," he said, carefully handing it over. "I'd very much like you to wear it again. Mr. Kent—"

"Oh, please, sir, call me Jeff."

"All right, Jeff. Would you come over here and help my daughter put this on?"

"Er...sure."

Susanna bit her lip to keep it from trembling, and held her breath as Jeff stood close behind her and fumbled with the necklace's tiny lock. Every nerve and cell was aquiver at his nearness as her senses took him in. The smell of him, clean, and vaguely spicy. The heat of him, radiating from his body and eagerly absorbed by hers. The feel of him, of his knuckles brushing sensitized skin...

Jeff knew that Susanna was holding her hair off her neck to help him see better what his fingers were doing. Unfortunately, the sight of her pale-skinned, delicately curved and vulnerable nape accomplished just the opposite. It took all his concentration and willpower not to press his lips against that tender spot.

As a result, his hands became all thumbs. They shook, and his nostrils quivered as Susanna's subtly floral and utterly feminine scent reached out to him. Combined with the silken feel of her skin against his fingers, it conjured up powerful visions of her naked and in his arms.

Sure, the one night they had spent together on the same bed had been well chaperoned and celibate, but it had started a thirst in Jeffrey that only full possession of her could quench—if it could be quenched at all.

The more time he spent with Susanna, the more he began to doubt it.

The two parts of the lock finally joined, and Jeff stepped back with an explosive sigh of relief and regret. As he moved, his eyes met those of Susanna's father, and the expression in them made it clear to Jeff that he'd been keenly watched, weighed, and, after a long moment of very thorough eye contact...approved. Discomfited and feeling oddly guilty, Jeff returned to his seat.

Over dinner the conversation inevitably got around to the troubles they'd encountered, and to Igor Otrovsky's demise.

"I've been in contact with the agency back in Seattle," Barney said, spearing a stalk of succulent imported white asparagus and contemplating it thoughtfully. "To all intents and purposes, sir, with Otrovsky out of the picture and the Iron Curtain a thing of the past, there's no reason you couldn't get back to being Harry Miller again."

Susanna, who had been thinking about that very thing, looked at her father expectantly.

He was smiling, a wistful half smile that tugged at her heartstrings and made her reach out and cover his hand with her own.

Harry sent her a glance that said he appreciated her support, and turned his gaze to their joined hands. "Yes," he said heavily, "they talked to me about that, too. You'd think I'd be glad, wouldn't you, knowing it was finally all over. But you know something?"

His mouth twisted and he shook his head. "It saddens me that Otrovsky had to be killed. Oh, I know it was necessary, Detective Golding. You did what you had to do or he would certainly have shot Jeffrey here in the back. And then he would have tried for me. Again."

Miller absently stroked his useless legs, shaking his head as if unable to understand the regret he felt. "And yet," he continued slowly, "he was always a worthy adversary. His death is the end of an era. An era in which I was young."

Sighing, he shook his head again, dismissing the mood. "As for my name..."

He turned to Susanna. "I became Frank King more than twenty years ago, after the shooting that left me with these mangled legs."

At her gasp of dismay, Harry reassuringly squeezed her hand. "It's all right, my dear. It's all ancient history by now and I've become quite reconciled to being on wheels rather than on foot. Everyone spoils me rotten—''

"And I will, too," Susanna said fervently, "for as long as you want. Forever."

"Oh no, you won't." Her father shook his forefinger in playful admonition. "I've got better plans than that for you, my girl. After we've had a nice, long visit and the legalities for your citizenship have been taken care of—I've already initiated the necessary proceedings—I expect you to get yourself hitched to someone like that nice young man you brought along."

Harry nodded approvingly toward Jeffrey, whose mouthful of prime rib suddenly refused to go down; he met Susanna's stricken look with barely concealed discomfiture.

"And get busy producing grandchildren. That reminds me," the older man added for Jeff's benefit in a more businesslike tone. "Let's have a brandy in the library after dinner."

Jeff inclined his head and refused to look at Barney, seated across the table.

"But we've digressed," Harry Miller went on, leaning back in his chair, hands folded across his middle and his gaze once again on his daughter.

"About being named King. After more than twenty years, I've just about gotten used to the name, but in my heart I've always remained Harry Miller. I've had a good life, everything considered. Better than yours and Maria's. Believe me, Susanna. . . ."

He paused, compressing his lips, and when he spoke again, his voice had roughened. "If I could have spared both of you the hardships you suffered, if I could have brought you over here the way I always wanted, I'd gladly have given up more than just my legs."

"I wouldn't have let you," Susanna said fervently. "Without you, what good would have been anything else?"

"Oh, what a daughter." Her father's expression grew tender. "What balm you are for an old man's soul." They gazed fondly at each other, then Miller said, "I can't tell you how happy it makes me to have you here, Susanna. To know you're finally in this country, here with me. You're the best thing I've ever done. I, Joseph Harrison Miller, and your mother, Maria Antonia Herz, we are your parents. Those were our names when you were conceived, and if I'd been able to, Miller would have been the name I'd have given both of you. And so—"

He took Susanna's hands and held them in his. "While I think it's too late for me to go back to being Harry Miller officially, I want you to have that name. Your father's name. Until the day of your wedding, anyway, when your name will be changed to—"

His gaze swerved and settled on Jeff "—something else."

Chapter Ten

Jeffrey was in the library with Susanna's father. It was a dark-paneled, very masculine room that obviously served as a study, as well. Two of the four walls were lined from floor to ceiling with books, expensive ones, judging by the gold-lettered leather spines that faced the room. A third wall was dominated by a fireplace in which, as had been the case in the living room, a log fire crackled and hissed. The sound and smell should have made the atmosphere more comfortable, but the truth was, Jeff had never felt more *un*comfortable in his life.

He was standing in front of that fire, staring at an enlarged painting of the same photograph that was in Susanna's gold, heart-shaped locket. Maria Jaeger. Maria Antonia Herz. Susanna's mother.

Studying her unsmiling, regular features, Jeff's back was toward his host, who had pulled his wheelchair to a massive, mahogany desk; Jeff could all but feel his eyes drilling holes between his shoulder blades.

Maria had been pretty, he noted distractedly, and an undeniable intelligence shone like a beacon from her light blue eyes. There was warmth there, he supposed, making allowances for the fact that no living person had sat for this portrait. The rich golden-blond waves framing her face in a sort of pageboy style were attractive. But overall, the woman seemed rather unremarkable. Certainly she hadn't been a Mata Hari type, or a glamor puss one might imagine dabbling in the kind of intrigue and espionage that had been Harry Miller's métier, nor did she seem dramatic enough to have inspired the sort of grand passion she and Harry Miller had apparently shared.

"The picture doesn't do her justice." Susanna's father spoke as if he'd read Jeffrey's thoughts. "In life, Maria was much more beautiful, infinitely more vibrant. Her maiden name, Herz, means 'heart,' you know, in German. It was very apt. She was all heart, all goodness. Too much so, I often thought, because it made her vulnerable to the kind of pain—"

He stopped and cleared his throat. Jeff turned slowly to face him, and was shaken by the naked anguish he saw in Harry Miller's eyes.

"I couldn't send for her or even contact her," Harry said bitterly. "Too much was at stake. They—that's our side—spouted off to me about national security, patriotism and all the other slogans designed to keep us waving the flag. I was loyal to our cause, still am— but I can't help but ask myself at what cost? At what price?"

Miller drew a deep, ragged breath and shifted his gaze to Jeff. "What has Susanna told you about her life over there?"

Jeff shrugged. "Not much, but enough to convince me that she spent most of her days dreaming of a real home and family."

Miller nodded; his lips tightened. "It's all my fault."

"Susanna never blamed you for anything."

Miller laughed without humor. "Which merely proves that she's a nice person, not that I'm blameless." He stared into the fire. "What else has she told you?"

Jeff absently picked up an amber paperweight and hefted it while his mind carefully weighed his reply. The longer he talked and listened to Harry Miller, the more he was growing to like and respect the man and to care. Just as being with and talking to Susanna had gradually, inexorably, drawn him to her. Tied him to her.

But all that had to stop, he told himself, and stop now, before he found himself bound to her—and to her father—so tightly, there'd be no way of pulling free.

"About what?" he prevaricated, despising himself for begging the question like that, but determined, with something akin to desperation, to establish some distance between them, to keep the conversation from growing any more personal. He was feeling all sorts of troubling vibrations from this far from incapacitated man in the wheelchair. But this man also happened to be the father of the woman Jeffrey...*desired* above all others, but...

That undefined, unspoken "but" very much troubled Jeff. He sensed that Harry Miller knew about it, too, and was curious to hear more.

"About her expectations," Harry replied with an edge to his voice. "About what she wants from life. From *me*, and..."

He paused until Jeff met his gaze, then said, "And what she expects from you."

For long moments their gazes held. Jeff was determined not to be the first to look away. He had nothing to hide, he told himself self-righteously. Susanna could have no expectations where he was concerned; he had made her no promises. And he had done nothing to this man's daughter that he needed to feel apologetic about.

So why did he feel apologetic?

Because he didn't know why, but couldn't shake the irrational feeling of guilt, Jeff knew he sounded irritable when he replied. "Susanna wants what all of us want. Parents, or *a* parent—to love us. Happiness, security. She wants to belong, to find a home."

"With me?"

A leading question, if ever Jeff had heard one. He bit hard on the insides of his cheeks and inwardly counted to three. When he could trust his voice to be firm and even, he said, "Yes, of course, with you. After all, you're all the family she's got."

Silence. Quite a lengthy one, during which neither of the men moved so much as an eyelash as they took each other's measure once again.

Jeff was still left with the conviction that, though he might not be able to walk, Joseph Harrison Miller was far from incapacitated. There was an aura of strength and power around him, and Jeff knew the man would be a formidable enemy. But—and of this, too, Jeff was sure—he'd be an equally committed ally.

What was Harry Miller thinking? There was nothing in his expression to give a clue.

"I see," was all he said after a while.

Jeff compressed his lips, struggling against the totally ridiculous feeling that he'd somehow dropped several notches in the older man's esteem, and the maddening realization that this really bothered him. With a curt nod he turned his back and made a show of studying another picture.

"My parents," Harry soberly supplied from behind him. "Both long dead but married fifty-nine years. Never had a damn thing in common except me, their only son, and the love they had for each other. Pop was a republican, Mother a flaming liberal. She was a blue blood, while he'd fought his way out of the Bowery...."

He let the sentence trail away, then said brusquely, "You have no intention of marrying Susanna, do you?"

The question came at Jeff so completely out of left field that for a moment he had no answer. He should have expected it, or some variation, of course. After all, at dinner Susanna's father had alluded to marriage and grandchildren quite meaningfully, and Jeff suspected that finding out his "intentions" had been the reason Miller had invited him into the library in the first place.

All right.

Drawing in a lungful of air, he braced himself and turned. "Actually," he said, as his vague sense of guilt and depression intensified, "the fact is, no, I don't. It's, ah, it's not like that between your daughter and me. Susanna and I are, well, we're friends, of course, but..."

There was that insidious "but" again.

Feeling totally inadequate and emotionally drained, Jeff dropped into the deep, leather-upholstered chair facing the desk and, pushing up his glasses, wearily pinched the bridge of his nose.

"Aw, hell," he said finally, hoarsely, after the silence in the room had grown as thick as the fog on the Oregon coast. Letting his specs drop back into place, he raised his head to look squarely into the hooded eyes of the older man across from him.

"I love her."

Very slowly, Harry Miller nodded. His lips quirked into something that wasn't quite a smile, but more an expression of empathetic understanding and wisdom. "I know. You probably don't think so, but it's quite obvious." He paused a beat. "It's just as obvious that Susanna loves you."

Heated denial on his lips, Jeff half surged out of the chair, only to immediately drop back into it. What could he say? Miller was right. Susanna might not have told him so in words, but her feelings had been there for Jeff to see. In her actions, in the trust she'd placed in him. In her touch, in her smile, in her eyes.

"I'm not what she needs," he said tiredly.

"Probably not."

"I'm a foreign correspondent, for God's sake. I'm never in one place for more than a year, and more often than not, the places I'm in are hellholes, trouble spots, the sewers of society even seasoned news hounds like me get sick in . . . and of. . . .''

"Life's a bitch," Miller murmured. "Isn't that the expression nowadays? Well," he added more forcefully, pushing himself away from the desk and wheeling the chair toward the door. "That's that, then. A damn shame, but I know what you're saying and I appreciate your candor. Don't forget, I'm the guy who's been there and beyond. It's the dregs, the pits, the worst. And yet . . ."

He was at the door now, one hand on the handle, his eyes steady on Jeff's. "And yet, though the excitement of it is like a drug in your blood and you think there's no way you can ever live without it, take it from me—" he opened the door "—you *can*. The love of that one special woman, on the other hand . . ."

Sighing, he let the sentence hang, and gave Jeff a parting nod. "I wish you a good night, Mr. Kent, and a safe trip back to Seattle."

And with that the door clicked shut behind the wheelchair and Jeff found himself alone. But not for long. His thoughts and emotions were still very much in turmoil when, moments later, Barney barged in.

"For Pete's sake, Kent, can we get out of here or what?"

Jeff looked up, bemused. "What?"

"Can we leave, hit the road, vamoose?" Barney growled impatiently. "What are you, deaf? If we wanna get outa this town at 4:00 a.m. as planned, let's go get us a damn hotel room and hit the sack. I'm dead on my feet, and Miller has gone to bed."

"Susanna . . . ?"

"I left her out on the patio a minute ago." Barney peered at the picture of Maria. "This her mother?"

"Yeah." Susanna was on the patio. Was she waiting for him to come and say goodbye? She knew he and Barney were leaving for Seattle first thing in the morning; they'd talked about it over dinner, and she'd been very quiet ever since.

Jeff knew he should go to her, say his farewells and get it over with. Maybe tell her... What? What was there possibly left for him to say?

"Doesn't look like her," Barney remarked, still studying the painting. "Except, maybe it does. I mean it's more like a feeling. Anyway—"

He turned and touched the paperweight on Harry's desk. "That's some love story she and Miller had going. Shades o' Romeo and Juliet, tragic lovers and all that. Quite a guy, though, old Harry, don't you think?"

Eyes narrowed, Barney assessed his friend. "You're looking mighty down at the mouth. What'd he have to say to you?"

"Huh? Oh, nothing." All of a sudden Jeff couldn't wait to get out. It was urgent that he find Susanna, that he explain to her.... He headed for the door. "Listen, Barn. You go on without me. Book us into the nearest Holiday Inn and I'll catch you later, all right?"

"For crying out loud, Kent..."

"Later, Golding."

"But...!" Left staring at the closed door, Barney roundly swore, and then a slow grin dawned on his ruined face. It hurt his nose. The grin faded. And, storming out of the room, another cursing session commenced.

He found her sitting on a bench, scrunched on her tailbone, staring at barely visible stars. Not wanting to startle her, Jeff softly called her name. . . .

"Susanna . . ."

She didn't move, didn't turn. Jeff stayed where he was, a few steps away.

"It's hard to imagine," she said musingly, after a while, "that people all over the world look up at the same stars as these and make wishes."

"Is that what you're doing?" Jeff walked up to her but, not wishing to crowd her, sat down at the other end of the bench. "Making a wish?"

"No." She turned her head and looked at him then. "All the wishes I had have already come true, remember?"

"All?"

She regarded him steadily. "Yes."

"Coming to America and finding your father?"

"Yes."

Edging closer, he took her hand. She flinched, but didn't pull away. "And having been granted that, is there really nothing else you want?"

"Don't do this, Jeffrey." She tugged at her hand almost violently.

Jeff let it go and, restless, got up to pace. He raked a hand through his hair and turned to her. How could she not sense his agony? "Susanna—"

"No." She stood, too. "Please don't say any more." She brushed past him. "It's late. You'd better go."

"No, please." He caught her by the shoulders and held her in place. "Please, Susanna, listen to me. There's something I have to say to you, something important."

His eyes beseeched her and, after a long moment of indecision, Susanna wearily nodded. "All right, Jeffrey. I'll listen."

"Thank you." Releasing her, he walked away a few steps, keeping his back to her as he groped for the right words.

"I was married once," he finally blurted. "A long time ago. She, Jillian, wasn't like you at all. Except in one way...."

He paused, waiting for Susanna to speak, and when she didn't, turned toward her. She was standing very still; only her eyes, large and incredibly sad, seemed to be alive in her face.

"She, too, needed what you need, Susanna," Jeff went on after a while. "She wanted to put down roots. She longed for security. She wanted a home, family...."

Even now, after nearly seven years, Jeff almost choked on the bitter pill of failure. He tipped back his head and looked at the stars as he tried to swallow the emotions he had worked so hard to run from and forget—regret, guilt, remorse for what he now knew had been his egocentrism, his selfishness. The same selfishness he was still guilty of.

He lowered his head and slanted a glance toward Susanna who stood as if carved in stone. "She never found what she needed with me, Susanna. I was unable—*unwilling*—to compromise. I wanted only what *I* wanted, which was to have total freedom to pursue my own dreams and wishes and to hell with anyone else. I made her unhappy, Susanna. I made her lonely. Much lonelier than she ever was before she hooked up with me."

Exasperated by Susanna's stillness, needing *something* from her—curses, recriminations, absolution? Anything but this poker-faced silence—Jeff strode to her and gripped her upper arms.

"Damn it, Susanna!" He gave her a little shake. "Don't you see what I'm saying? Don't you hear me? I'm the same selfish bastard now that I was then. I'm no good for you, no good at settling down!"

"Have I asked you to?" He'd never heard a voice so cold.

Chilled by it, he released her and fumbled for words. "Well, no. But—"

"And is that all you've come out here to say to me?"

"You're angry with me." He couldn't stand this indifference. "All I wanted was for you to understand."

"And I do." She relented and gave him a sad smile. "I really do. And I thank you for everything you've given me, Jeffrey. Sincerely. I will always be in your debt."

"Don't." Impatient now, he waved her thanks away and caught her hands. "You're upset and I don't want us to part this way. Susanna," he said urgently, "remember what we said back in Beecham?"

She nodded, blinking back tears.

"Friends, remember?"

"Yes," she whispered huskily, nodding again. "Friends." Rising, she kissed him on the cheek, then tugged her hands out of his and stepped back. "I'm afraid friendship is no longer enough for me, however. I'm sorry and . . . goodbye, Jeffrey."

Wanting to stop her, knowing he couldn't, Jeffrey stood by the bench in Harry Miller's compound and watched the woman he loved walk out of his life.

Susanna had longed for her father all of her days, with a yearning so strong and abiding that after her mother's death, it had been the force which had given her life a new direction. Every one of her actions—study, work, scrimp, save—had been deliberate steps toward the goal of one day making it possible to find Joseph Harrison Miller, to go to him and be with him.

Yet now all the things that had driven her throughout those long, dark and often despairing years in East Germany, all the yearning and sometimes the despair, seemed like nothing compared to the intensity with which she yearned for Jeffrey Kent.

It was Christmas Eve. Two weeks had passed since she had driven with Jeff and Barney Golding through her father's imposing gates, two weeks since that evening when, after dinner, her father and Jeffrey had gone into the library, and Barney had asked her to walk with him in the huge, magical grounds that surrounded the house. Two weeks of waiting, though not of idling; two weeks of hoping, even as she made plans to move out of her father's house and took steps to find a job.

Two weeks without a word from Jeff.

Barney had clearly been wrong.

"Happy now?" he had asked Susanna that night, walking with her beneath the swaying palms.

"Yes," she'd said. "Very." But the note of wistfulness had been audible, even to her own ears, and Barney, being a policeman and used to listening to things *unsaid* as well as said, must have heard it, too.

"It's Jeff, isn't it?" he asked, more kindly than Susanna had ever heard him speak. "You love him."

Her little laugh was half a sob. "That transparent, am I?"

He shrugged. "Reading people and looking past the fronts they put up is my job."

They walked in silence for a while. The air had turned crisp; the sky was cloudless, but too bright with the reflected city lights to let stars be visible. Still, looking around, Susanna thought how much more beautiful everything was than she'd ever imagined, and condemned herself for being ungrateful, for wanting still more.

Jeffrey...

"He's crazy about you, you know." Barney sat down on a bench and patted the spot next to him.

Susanna sat, crossing her legs and clasping her hands around one knee. "I know he wants me." She found talking with Barney easy, especially here, in the near darkness of her father's garden. "We, uh, we would have made love on this journey, except..."

"Except I showed up."

His dry tone made her laugh. "You and everybody else, it would seem." She sobered. "Which should probably tell me that things between Jeffrey and me just aren't meant to be."

"Bull."

"I take it you don't believe in predestination," Susanna said, amused again in spite of her heartache.

Barney snorted. "Hardly. Gimme facts, gimme hard evidence. With you and Kent the fact is you two are—" He stopped and winced. "I hate the term *in love*, but that's what you are, and the evidence ... hell, you don't have to be a cop to see the evidence. All anybody has to do is look at the two o' you together."

"But Jeffrey—"

"Is an idiot, but not stupid. I'm tellin' ya, let the guy go. Good riddance. Give him some time to figure things out. Let him miss you. And while he's doing that, you, young lady, relax and have a good time. Enjoy your Dad, your new home." Slapping his knees, Barney hoisted himself to his feet. "Take my word for it, kid, Kent'll be back."

Barney had sounded so sure that Susanna had believed him. But now it had been two weeks....

Feeling her father's eyes on her, she carefully hung the last piece of tinsel and stepped away from the small, perfectly shaped fir she had placed upon a low corner table and lovingly trimmed. There had been no holiday decorations of any kind in the house. For just himself, Harry had never felt the need to bother.

He'd told her that he had always given his staff the holidays off, managing only with the help of a substitute nurse-companion. This year Susanna had, of course, insisted on taking over for Ross Cunningham. And so father and daughter were alone to celebrate their first Christmas together.

Forcing cheer into her voice, Susanna presented her handiwork with a elegant flick of the wrist. "Well? What do you think?"

"Magnificent." Harry rolled himself closer, took his daughter's hand and kissed it affectionately. "A masterpiece." Releasing her, he moved toward the door. "The only things missing are the presents, and I just happen to have a couple tucked away in the library. Be right back."

"Me, too." Susanna had brought an old studio photo of Maria and herself from Germany, and with Meyer, the butler's, assistance had had it set in an antique silver frame. She ran up to her room to get it, and was placing the beautifully wrapped package beneath the tree when her father returned with several boxes of his own.

"Now I know you said you wanted us to do Christmas in typical American fashion," he said, "opening presents on Christmas morning and all that. Which is fine. But here's one—" he handed her the largest box of all "—that simply can't wait.

"Go on," he encouraged, when Susanna eyed first the box and then him with obvious reluctance. "Don't be a spoilsport. Opening a special present or two on Christmas Eve is an American tradition, too."

"Well, all right, then." Pulling a chair up close to her father, Susanna suddenly felt about ten years old and very excited. Presents had been few and far between in her life, and this one, though not very heavy, suddenly had the feel of something very special, indeed.

Hands not quite steady, she carefully removed the bow and ribbons, ignoring her father's amused admonition to hurry. "These are too pretty to ruin," she said. "And look at this paper!"

As if the wrapping were the gift, she oohed and aahed and carefully folded the paper before opening the cardboard box inside. It contained another, slightly smaller box, also wrapped.

A quick glance into her father's tenderly twinkling eyes, and she set about unwrapping that one with exactly the same care she'd used on the first. And found another box inside.

Charmed, she clapped her hands. "A trick gift. I love it!"

She pressed a quick kiss onto her father's cheek and set to work again. In all, there were six boxes to be unwrapped, and in the final, very small one, lay a folded piece of paper.

Go out onto the terrace, said the message in her father's hand.

Susanna jumped to her feet with a delighted laugh. "What fun!" And was halfway across the living room before she called back, "Well, aren't you coming?"

"No, I'll wait here," Harry said, with a hoarseness in his tone that hadn't been there before.

"Father." Susanna was instantly back by his side, all her laughter forgotten. "What is it? A sore throat?"

She began to feel for his glands, but he gently pushed her hands away. "I'm fine. Just a little choked up at seeing you so happy."

Then she saw the sheen of moisture in his eyes, and her own filled in response. "Oh, Father." Kneeling, she hugged him close. "I love you."

"And I love you." He hugged her back, then gently pushed her away. "Now go out on that terrace and get your present."

"All right. I'll bring it right in."

"Take your time. Enjoy."

Nodding, she called back a light, "Thank you," and stepped out onto the large, slate-floored terrace.

The lights at each corner of the balustrade had clearly been put there for decoration and atmosphere rather than illumination. Their meager radiance served only to make the pockets of darkness between them seem even darker.

Casting around for some gift-wrapped container of sorts, or a note, Susanna saw nothing but the outdoor furniture, with the umbrella folded down.

Her quick, uncertain look back at her father was met with an encouraging nod, so, taking a deep breath, she walked to the railing and carefully made her way along it from one light to the next. All the time she carefully looked around, feeling for a tacked-on piece of paper that might contain a further clue.

She had just stepped into the deepest pocket of darkness when she heard a scraping noise from behind her, as if someone had pushed back a chair.

Whirling, her eyes widened. A gasp gathered in her throat, but never got out. It was swallowed, thoroughly eaten up by a kiss so hot and devouring, all her senses burst into flame.

Jeffrey.

His name was the only coherent thought Susanna was able to formulate for quite some time. Jeff was kissing her, and she was kissing him, as if neither ever wanted to stop. Barely coming up for air, heads slanting this way and that, they sought for an ever deeper joining. Mouths open, tongues now entwined, now rhythmically stroking, they feasted. Teeth nipped.

Hands gripped, searched and held on tight as their bodies strained.

Panting, they broke apart, just long enough for Jeff to say in a raspy voice, "Lord, but I love you, girl!"

Susanna's "And I love you," nearly suffered the same fate as her gasp had earlier. But not quite. Jeff had heard the words and was once again kissing her with hungry intensity.

"Merry Christmas," he said, when at last they could bear to be an inch or two apart.

Susanna felt her eyes grow round. "You mean—"

"Yup." He grinned, dropping a kiss onto her nose. "I'm it. Your present." He moved his head back a bit to peer into her face. "Disappointed?"

"Well . . ." she began teasingly, giddy with happiness, but found herself kissed into silence before she could say more.

"Marry me, Susanna." Jeff's voice was rough, his tone urgent now. "I've been such a jerk, such a blind fool. I don't want to travel anymore, not if it means leaving you. I love you. And I want to make a home for you. *With* you. I want us to have kids, be a family. I want—God, Susanna, I want *you*. Only you. All the time, day and night.

"My sweetheart." He kissed her greedily. "Marry me, love. My life is empty without you in it." They kissed again. "These past two weeks have been hell."

"For me, too."

"Then marry me, Susanna."

"Oh, Jeffrey." All of her dreams were about to come true! Susanna closed her eyes against a rush of tears. A sob wrenched itself free from the tightness in her throat and she hid her face in the warmth of Jeffrey's neck.

His own lids prickling, and his throat feeling as though a brick had lodged itself sideways, Jeff held his beloved in his arms and let her cry. Standing with her like this, the feel of her body leaning into his so right and so good, he wondered how he could ever have doubted. How could he ever have had reservations about joining his life to this woman's?

The two weeks away from her had been agony, the thought of never seeing her again intolerable. Waiting for today, for *now*, had almost laid him low, in spite of all the frantic running around he'd been doing since going back to Seattle.

Gradually Susanna quieted and finally raised her head. "I'm sorry."

Jeff cleared his throat and gave her a lopsided grin. "What kind of answer is that to my proposal?"

With a sobbing little laugh, she struggled to punch him in the side. "I'm so happy," she said.

"I can see that." Using his thumbs, he wiped at her tears. Tenderness, not passion, filled him now. He ached with it as he gently kissed her lips and whispered, "I'll be happy, too, Susanna, as soon as you say you'll marry me."

"Oh, Jeffrey. My love." Reaching up, Susanna framed his face and looked at him with all the love in her heart. "I will. Of course, I will."

"January 2?"

"Jan—?"

"Your father's got everyone standing by."

"My fa—?"

"So has my mother." Jeff caught Susanna's lower lip and gently tugged on it with his teeth. "For the past week the telephone wires from Seattle to here have been completely tied up by our families."

Something stirred in Susanna; a spark of rebellion? "Pretty sure of yourself, weren't you?"

"No." Every hint of playfulness abruptly left Jeffrey's expression. He cupped her shoulders and held her away from him. "Not me. The only thing I've been sure of is that I love you and want you. I'm lonely and miserable without you, and I'm no longer the selfish idiot who couldn't stand to be tied down seven years ago. It was the others—your father and my mother most of all—who seemed completely certain about everything else."

"And I think I know why." Susanna laughed a little shakily. "I've been in touch with your mother, you see."

"Oh?" Now it was Jeff's turn to be taken aback.

"Yes." Stepping out of his light hold, Susanna turned to look over the shadowed grounds. "You see, thanks to Barney Golding's help, I've got several quite promising job interviews lined up in Seattle."

"Barney Golding, eh? Why, that son of a gun!"

"And your mother very kindly offered me my room back. Only until I'd found my own apartment, of course," she hastened to add after a quick sideways glance at Jeff; his brows had soared above his glasses.

"So you were moving to Seattle," he said slowly, reaching out and turning her to face him. "And why was that, Susanna?"

"Why—" Biting her lip, she tried not to smile. "To track you down, of course, you terrible man. To tell you I loved you and that you'd darn well better—"

"Make an honest woman out of you?" he finished. A grin of delight stretched his lips.

Equally delighted, Susanna grinned back. "Something like that."

"And when was this move to take place?" Drawing close again, they kissed.

"Day after tomorrow."

"I see." Jeff's hands explored the curve of Susanna's spine and came to rest on the pleasing swell below. "And isn't that too bad," he added after a bit of tender exploration and heavy breathing. "Because you see, the trouble is, you can't."

"Can't?" Susanna nuzzled his throat. "Why ever not?"

Growling his need, Jeff caught Susanna's sweetly marauding lips with his and feasted his fill. "Because," he said when they came up for air, "I'm moving here. To L.A."

When her jaw dropped open, he gently closed it with one finger. "I've quit my job, Susanna."

"Oh, Jeffrey, you didn't. You did? But . . . I mean, are you sure?"

"Very."

"But you said you loved the excitement!"

"I love you more." Jeff dropped a kiss onto her nose. "Besides, I'll get all the excitement I can handle from showing you the world, sweetheart. My world."

"Hmm." She smiled dreamily. "I'd like that."

"So would I." They kissed again, leisurely. "But first," Jeff said at last with a grimace, "I've got to find gainful employment again. Which is why I've got these interviews lined up here, you see." He smiled. "And you know something? Oddly enough, I, too, owe a couple of them to Barney Golding."

Looking into each other's eyes, they burst out laughing. "Who would've thought it?" Jeff gasped, when he could finally speak. "Barney Golding—playing Cupid."

They were still laughing at the image of a red-haired, cigar-chomping little rascal with wings and a quiver of arrows when Harry Miller spoke from the doorway.

"I trust, my dear daughter, all this hilarity means you liked the surprise gift I sent you out here to find."

"It does. Oh, yes, it does." Tugging Jeff along, Susanna went to her father and hunkered down in front of his chair. Taking his hand, she pressed it to her cheek. "Thank you, Father."

"Nonsense," Harry blustered. "A purely selfish act on my part. A man gets old, he wants grandchildren."

"We'll do our best to oblige as quickly as possible, sir," Jeff said, drawing Susanna into his arms. "Won't we, sweetheart?"

"Oh, yes, my love." She gazed into his eyes, showing him the world of love in hers. "Oh, yes, indeed, we will."

* * * * *

**Three All-American beauties discover
love comes in all shapes and sizes!**

ALL-AMERICAN SWEETHEARTS

by Laurie Paige

CARA'S BELOVED (#917)—*February*
SALLY'S BEAU (#923)—*March*
VICTORIA'S CONQUEST (#933)—*April*

A lost love, a new love and a hidden one, three *All-American
Sweethearts* get their men in Paradise Falls, West Virginia.
Only in America...and only from Silhouette Romance!

Silhouette
R O M A N C E™

$\mathcal{S}$ SPRING FANCY

Three bachelors, footloose and fancy-free... until now!

Spring into romance with three fabulous fancies by three of Silhouette's hottest authors:

ANNETTE BROADRICK
LASS SMALL
KASEY MICHAELS

When spring fancy strikes, no man is immune!

Look for this exciting new short-story collection in March at your favorite retail outlet.

Only from

where passion lives.

INTIMATE MOMENTS®

10TH Anniversary

Celebrate our anniversary with a fabulous collection of firsts....

The first Intimate Moments titles written by three of your favorite authors:

NIGHT MOVES   Heather Graham Pozzessere
LADY OF THE NIGHT   Emilie Richards
A STRANGER'S SMILE   Kathleen Korbel

Silhouette Intimate Moments is proud to present a FREE hardbound collection of our authors' firsts—titles that you will treasure in the years to come from some of the line's founding members.

This collection will not be sold in retail stores and is available only through this exclusive offer. Look for details in Silhouette Intimate Moments titles available in retail stores in May, June and July.

SIMANN

HE'S MORE THAN A MAN, HE'S ONE OF OUR

DAD GALAHAD
by Suzanne Carey

Confirmed bachelor Ned Balfour hadn't thought of himself as a knight in shining armor—until he met Jenny McClain. The damsel in distress had turned to Ned for help, and his sense of duty wouldn't let him disappoint the fair maiden. Jenny's baby needed a father and he vowed to become that man, even though mother and child would surely disrupt his solitary life. Could this ready-made family be the answer to Ned's quest for happiness?

Find out who does the true rescuing in Suzanne Carey's DAD GALAHAD. Available in April—only from Silhouette Romance!

Fall in love with our FABULOUS FATHERS—and join the Silhouette Romance family!

Silhouette ROMANCE™

COMING NEXT MONTH

#928 DAD GALAHAD—Suzanne Carey
Fabulous Fathers
It was Ned Balfour to the rescue for damsel in distress
Jenny McClain. Pregnant and alone, Jenny accepted Ned's
chivalrous offer of marriage, but could she trust this white
knight with her heart?

#929 WHO'S THAT BABY?—Kristin Morgan
Whitney Arceneaux was irresistibly drawn to both her new
neighbor, Garrett Scott, and his precious toddler. Yet there was
something *very* strange about this man—and the need she felt for
them both....

#930 LYON'S PRIDE—Maris Soule
Cartoonist Greg Lyon had taken a journey to find himself but
he discovered Dr. Amy Fraser instead. Though she'd cured his
injured leg with ease, he knew *he'd* have to be the one to mend
her heart.

#931 SORRY, WRONG NUMBER—Patricia Ellis
When a wrong number introduced Meg Porter to Nick Morgan, it
was a strong case of love on the line. But would Meg accept Nick
for who he really was, once they met face-to-face?

#932 THE RIGHT MAN—Marie Ferrarella
Leanne Sheridan had survived one bad marriage and was not
about to get involved with Cody Lancaster. Leanne's mind was
convinced Cody was all wrong for her...but her heart insisted he
was Mr. Right!

#933 VICTORIA'S CONQUEST—Laurie Paige
All-American Sweethearts
Lovely widow Victoria Broderick was intrigued by the depth of
passion Jason Broderick hid from the world. Now all she had to
do was make him admit his feelings for *her!*